BENEATH THE CROWN: WHEN LOYALTY COSTS TOO MUCH

MICHELLE CRUMBLE-SHARPE

Published by Jacinth Media Productions LLC
jacinthmediaproductions.com | info@JacinthMediaProductions.com

ISBN 978-1-960594-50-1 (Paperback)
ISBN 978-1-960594-51-8 (Hardback)
ISBN 978-1-960594-52-5 (eBook)

Cover and interior design: Jacinth Media Productions LLC
Edited by Jacinth Media Productions LLC

Printed in the United States of America

CONTENTS

Dedication

This book is dedicated to everyone who has ever carried **loyalty heavier than wisdom,** to those who **lost themselves while trying to hold others together,** and to **anyone learning that healing begins the moment you choose yourself.**

"What does it profit a man to gain the whole world, yet forfeit his soul?"

-Mark 8:36

CHAPTER 1

The Crown of Luck

The rain tapped a rhythmic prayer against the fogged window of the small-town diner, a steady weeping from the heavens that mirrored the saturation of my own soul. Outside, the streetlights shimmered in oily puddles, but inside, the only light that mattered was the flickering fluorescent bulb humming above booth three—Crystal's booth. I had been coming here every morning for months, sipping the cheapest coffee on the menu, tucking myself into the corner like a ghost with nowhere else to haunt. In my hand sat a crumpled lottery ticket. My fingers had worn the edges soft, the paper feeling like a fragile leaf shed in the winter of my life. I hadn't scratched it yet. Not because I didn't want to know, but because I couldn't handle another loss. When the soil of your life is dry and cracked, you fear the very water that might save you. Six months unemployed. A maxed-out credit card. A disconnected phone line. My silence was my shield, a heavy armor I wore to keep the world from seeing the roots of my desperation.

I looked out the window, my reflection ghosting over the rain-streaked glass. My son, Deon, had just declared for the NBA Draft. He was the fruit of my labor, the one green branch in a forest I feared was burning down. He was in California now—6'5", disciplined, hungry for a life that didn't taste like nickel coffee and broken promises. He had made it out of our neighborhood, pushing past the whispers of those who only saw the dirt he came from and not the height of his potential. He climbed past the doubters and the cold stares from coaches who didn't think boys like him had the stamina to bloom in the bright lights.

I had followed him west. Quietly. I was a mother in the shadows, a root system supporting the tree from beneath the earth, clapping the loudest but speaking the softest. No one at the gym knew I was broke. No one knew I had spent my last hundred dollars on a one-way Greyhound to Los Angeles, sitting upright for three days as the landscape shifted from the familiar to the unknown. No one knew I had a lottery ticket burning a hole in my wallet—a paper thin hope against a mountain of debt.

But they loved me. The staff at the gym, the other parents—they called me "Mama Crown." It was a name I didn't understand at first, until I realized it came from the way I sat in the stands. I carried my head high, an internal dignity that refused to bow even when the wind of poverty tried to break my spirit. I sat as if I wore gold, even when my pockets were filled with nothing but lint and faith. I didn't look like a woman on the edge of collapse; I looked like a woman who knew that a crown isn't just something you wear, but something you protect.

And then, the winter came early. One day, I didn't show up. Not for Deon's practice. Not for lunch at the diner. Not for the early-morning affirmations I whispered to him in the tunnel before he took the court—those words of life meant to armor him against the world. I was in a hospital bed, the air turned to lead as COVID drained the color from my skin and the oxygen from my lungs. My husband was in the next room, fighting the same silent fire. Our son missed critical tryouts to be with us, his future flickering in the balance of our breath. He stayed strong for our sake, his voice trembling as he whispered our own affirmations back to us through a phone screen. But I could see the wilting in his eyes. The pain showed in his game. He played with hesitation, his movements heavy as if the soil of his heart had turned to mud. The scouts noticed. They saw a player distracted, not realizing they were watching a son trying to hold his world together with a prayer.

My voice cracked every time I tried to reach for the Heavens. *Lord, let this cup pass,* I would whisper, the scripture a dry stone in my mouth. All I had left was that lottery ticket in my purse on the nightstand and the stubborn, bone-deep belief that we hadn't come this far to be uprooted by a season of sickness.

Three weeks later, weak but alive, I returned to the diner. My body felt like a brittle reed, but my spirit was beginning to reach for the sun again. I took my spoon and slowly scratched the card. The silver curled like ash, floating softly to the table like the remnants of a fire that had finally burned itself out.

My breath caught. The numbers aligned like stars in a clear night sky. "Jackpot," I whispered, the word tasting like the first rain after a drought.

The waitress—a kind woman named Shirley who had seen my darkest mornings—tilted her head from across the counter. "You okay, hon? You look like you've seen a miracle."

I smiled through tears, my hand resting over the ticket, feeling the weight of the crown settling firmly back onto my head. "I think I just bought my son his second chance. The roots held, Shirley. The roots held."

CHAPTER 2

SHELTER AND SISTERHOOD

When I returned home to North Carolina, the million-dollar check in my purse felt heavier than the Greyhound ticket ever had. It wasn't the weight of the paper, but the weight of stewardship—the realization that God had finally provided the rain for a long-dormant harvest. My first instinct wasn't to call a banker or a lawyer to shield my new perimeter. Instead, I reached for the person who had been part of my root system when the soil was nothing but dust and rocks. I called Emily.

We had grown up together—two girls navigating the thorny path of womanhood in a small town that didn't always make it easy for flowers like us to bloom. When I lost my parents and felt like a sapling ripped from the earth, it was Emily's family who brought me in, replanting me in the warmth of their own home. Years later, when Emily brought her first baby into the world, I was the one standing in the delivery room, holding her hand and witnessing the miracle of a new branch on her family tree.

We were more than friends. We were soul sisters, our lives intertwined like the vines of a great wisteria, holding each other up as we climbed toward the light.

The rain followed me from the diner to my doorstep, a persistent reminder that even the most beautiful seasons begin with a storm. When Emily answered my door that gray afternoon, the "Calm Mentor" in me knew the signs of a soul under siege. She stood there with two heavy duffel bags at her feet—her life packed into nylon and zippers—and tear-streaked cheeks hidden beneath the protective brim of her hat.

I didn't need to ask why the wind had blown her my way. I simply opened the door wide, my heart expanding with the space I now had to offer.

"Come in, sister," I said, my voice a steady anchor. "Stay as long as you need. My house is your greenhouse now."

In the weeks that followed, the house transformed. Our kids, once inseparable as toddlers, picked up right where they had left off, their footsteps a rhythmic percussion against the floorboards. Laughter filled the rooms again—raucous, echoing, healing laughter that acted like sunlight on a wilted garden. We shared coffee in the quiet, misty mornings and leaned into the honesty of wine at night. It felt like a second chance wrapped in a warm blanket of shared memory and newfound trust.

One night, while the steam from a pot of leftover spaghetti rose like incense between us, Emily sat at the table flipping through social media, her face illuminated by the blue light of the screen. I watched her, noticing the way her spirit was beginning to straighten, her own internal crown settling back into place. She stopped scrolling and sighed, the sound heavy with a vision.

"I keep thinking," she said, swirling the deep red liquid in her glass, her eyes fixed on something I couldn't yet see. "About what we could do with this season, Crystal. Something meaningful. Something that helps other women find their footing in the dirt."

I leaned back, the "Mama Crown" in me listening for the heartbeat behind her words. "Like what, Em?"

"A dental tech school," she said, the spark in her eyes catching like a match. "It's a growing field. I've taught the curriculum before; I know the bones of it. You've got the seeds—the funds—now. We could build something. A place of refuge and education for women who are where we used to be. For people like us who just need someone to believe in their bloom."

I nodded slowly, feeling the resonance of her words in my chest. It was a Proverbs 27:17 moment—*iron sharpening iron*. My resources and her expertise were two parts of a whole, ready to be grafted together.

"You bring the credentials," I told her, my voice thick with the certainty of a woman who had seen miracles in the mud. "I'll bring the bank account. Let's build a nursery for the dreams of others."

That night, the dinner table became a sanctuary of strategy. We scribbled ideas on paper napkins, the ink bleeding into the thin white squares as we mapped out curriculum ideas, names that sounded like strength, and locations that felt like home.

It didn't feel like a business transaction. It didn't feel like a cold corporate venture.

It felt like destiny taking root.

CHAPTER 3

DREAMS WITH BLUEPRINTS

The week that followed felt like a whirlwind of wind and light, a sudden season of growth where everything that had been dormant began to push through the surface. One week later, we found ourselves standing in the sterile, fluorescent-lit halls of the county clerk's office, our hands trembling as we filed the paperwork for an LLC: **Crown Point Academy**.

The name had come to me in a dream, a whisper from the Spirit about the destiny we were tilling. It was "Crown" for the dignity we wanted to restore to every woman who had been told she was just the dirt beneath someone else's feet. It was "Point" because every woman needed one—a launching point to fly, a turning point to change direction, and a final point to stand tall and say: *I made it. I am still here.*

We found our "nursery" in a modest brick building near downtown. To a stranger's eye, it was a wreck—the walls were yellowed with the nicotine of old failures, and the carpet was stained like a field after a flood. But Emily and I didn't see the decay; we saw the fallow ground. We spent fourteen-hour days reclaiming that space. We painted the walls a shimmering ivory, a clean slate for new beginnings, and hung motivational posters in heavy gold frames that caught the afternoon sun. In the front lobby, we placed a large, ornate mirror. Using a tube of bright red lipstick, I wrote across the glass in bold, looping letters: *You belong here.* I wanted every woman who walked through those doors to see her own reflection framed by the promise of her worth.

While Emily was the heart of the curriculum, I became the gardener of the operations. For a woman who had recently survived on the crumbs of a lottery ticket and the grace of a coffee shop booth, the world of business was a new kind of wilderness. I stayed up long after the kids were asleep, the blue light of my laptop screen illuminating the "Calm Mentor" I was becoming. I took online classes, my mind stretching to hold the complexities of filing permits, managing the ledger in QuickBooks, and navigating the digital harvest of social media marketing. Learning to manage the money felt like learning how to properly irrigate a field; I knew that if I didn't direct the flow correctly, the dream would wither.

Emily, meanwhile, was in her element. She revised her old lesson plans, her red pen flying across the pages as she infused her technical knowledge with the spirit of our mission. She recruited a few local instructors—women who, like us, knew that a job was more than a paycheck; it was a root system.

On the weekends, our children became our greatest ambassadors. They hit the sun-drenched streets, passing out flyers with the same hunger we felt, their laughter a melody that announced our arrival to the neighborhood. When we finally processed our first official enrollment, we didn't just file a paper—we celebrated a miracle. We sat on the floor of our half-finished lobby, feasting on tacos and sugar-dusted cupcakes, the crumbs falling onto the new carpet like confetti.

We weren't just building a school. We were building a legacy. We were planting a forest where others could finally find shade.

CHAPTER 4

BRICKS, BONDS, AND BUSINESS

The first year was a season of survival, a time of tilling hard, stubborn soil where every inch of progress had to be earned with sweat and prayer. We were like gardeners in a drought, carrying water by the thimbleful just to keep our young saplings alive. We didn't just lead; we labored. We taught the classes until our voices were raspy, then stayed late to clean the bathrooms and file mountains of paperwork. I remember the frustration of those late nights, my fingers stained with ink as I wrestled with printers that jammed every other day—machines that seemed as temperamental as the lives we were trying to help rebuild. But in the quiet of those midnight hours, I would look at the empty desks and whisper a prayer over them, calling forth the fruit I knew would one day grow there.

By the second year, the wheel of the season turned, and the seeds we had sown began to break the surface with undeniable momentum. The struggle started to bear the sweetness of recognition. Local news ran a story about "Two Women Lifting a Community," and suddenly, the whispers of our work became a roar. We were invited to a Chamber of Commerce banquet—a world of polished shoes and clinking crystal that felt a lifetime away from the Greyhound bus and the diner booth. They presented us with a plaque that caught the light, engraved with words that hummed in my spirit: *"For Service and Sisterhood."*

I cried when we returned to the school and nailed that plaque to the wall. It wasn't just metal and wood; it was a sign that the Crown was being restored, not just to us, but to the very building itself.

As we grew, our roles naturally settled into a beautiful rhythm. Emily became the vibrant face of the classroom. Her students absolutely loved her—she was sharp and structured, yet real enough to meet them in their pain. She was the bloom that everyone saw. I remained the root, handling the hidden business of grants, budgeting, and the digital harvest of marketing. I made sure the soil stayed nutrient-rich so her garden could flourish. We made a powerful pair, a testament to what happens when two women decide that their loyalty to a dream is worth the cost of the climb.

At our very first graduation ceremony, the air in the room felt thick with a holy electricity. A student named Tasha stood at the podium, her hands trembling as she gripped the edges of the wood. She looked out at us, her graduation cap sitting like a newly placed crown upon her head.

"I never thought I'd wear this," she said, her voice cracking as she touched the tassel. "I came here thinking I was worthless, a branch that had been snapped off and cast aside. But you saw the root. You believed in me when I was still buried in the dark. You gave me a place to grow."

In that moment, the "Mama Crown" in me felt a surge of such profound gratitude that it stole my breath. Emily and I reached for each other's hands, our fingers interlocking—a bond forged in the fire and strengthened by the rain. We stood there and wept, the tears washing away the exhaustion of the last two years, leaving behind only the joy of the harvest.

CHAPTER 5

UNEVEN GROUND

By the fourth year, the season began to turn, but not toward the warmth of summer. A subtle frost was creeping into the garden we had worked so hard to tend. Something had shifted in the soil of our partnership, a quiet tremors that suggested the ground beneath Crown Point Academy was no longer level.

Emily, who used to be the first to arrive, her spirit blooming with the sunrise, began arriving late. She cited vague family issues, her eyes avoiding mine as she hurried past the front desk. Our staff meetings, once a place of shared vision and prayerful planning, became curt and heavy. Her emails were clipped, stripped of the warmth that usually characterized our sisterhood. She no longer stayed after class to chat with students or share a glass of wine with me while we watched the sunset over the city. I felt the distance growing like a thicket of thorns between us, but as a "Mama Crown," I kept pushing through, telling myself it was just a long winter of the soul.

Then came the budget discrepancies—small, jagged holes in our financial safety net. I began to notice withdrawals labeled "community outreach," yet there was no explanation, no paper trail, and no new lives being touched by those funds. Receipts went missing. Accounts that should have been overflowing were suddenly overdrawn. The "Calm Mentor" in me tried to remain steady, but my spirit felt the first cold draft of betrayal.

When I finally brought it up—approaching her gently in the quiet of her office, my voice a soft plea for clarity—Emily waved it off with a sharp flick of her wrist.

"It's fine, Crystal. You're overthinking the numbers again," she said, her voice lacking its usual melody. "I'll get the invoices. You worry too much. We're doing good work; don't let a little paperwork cloud the vision."

I nodded, my lips offering a smile I didn't feel, but my gut didn't agree. My discernment—that still, small voice that had guided me through the hospital and the diner—was screaming that the roots were being poisoned.

I stayed up late that night, the house silent and heavy around me. I sat at my kitchen table, the same place where we had once scribbled dreams on napkins, and re-read our founding documents. I logged into the business accounts, my heart hammering against my ribs like a trapped bird. I looked at our mission statement, the words about "restoring dignity" and "integrity of the crown" mocking me from the page.

Something wasn't right. The fruit of our labor was being hollowed out from the inside. And for the first time since this journey began, I was afraid to ask how deep the rot went, or how wrong this beautiful dream could truly become.

CHAPTER 6

THE OTHER WEBSITE

It happened by accident, the way a sudden gust of wind might knock a dead branch from a tree just to show you where the rot began.

I have never been the type to pry. I have always believed that trust is the rich soil in which sisterhood grows, and I held a brand of loyalty that didn't require passwords or keys to prove its worth. My heart was an open gate. But that Tuesday afternoon, as the sun dipped low and cast long, skeletal shadows across the classroom floor, I found myself cleaning up after a long staff development day. While reaching for a stray pen under Emily's desk, my fingers brushed against something small and cold.

I pulled it out—a small black flash drive. It sat in my palm, unlabeled and silent. No name, no logo, just a plain device with a red cap that looked, in hindsight, like a tiny warning light. I figured it had simply slipped from Emily's tote during the day's rush. Without a second thought, I slipped it into my purse, intending to return it to my sister-friend the next morning.

The week grew heavy, and I forgot it was there. That Saturday, as a gentle rain tapped against my home office window, I sat down to catch up on the administrative reports that kept our "Crown" polished. I remembered the drive. I wasn't trying to snoop; I truly wasn't. I simply wondered if it held the training templates Emily had mentioned she was struggling to find. I thought I was helping the garden grow when I plugged it into my laptop.

The computer hummed to life, and my screen filled with folders—neatly named, professionally structured, and terrifyingly unfamiliar.

Not one folder bore the name "Crown Point Academy."

Instead, the screen was a sea of names that felt like ice water in my veins: *BrightSmile Training Institute, New Staff Orientation, Enrollment Forms 2025*, and a final folder that felt like a physical blow to my chest: *Logo Concepts - BS.*

I blinked, my eyes burning as I stared at the words. *BrightSmile?*

I clicked. My breath hitched as a full website mockup blossomed across the screen. It was crisp, modern, and vibrant. I scrolled through the course offerings and the tuition plans. It was our curriculum—the very one Emily and I had labored over, word for word, prayer for prayer. The same structure, the same flow, the same heartbeat. But the "Crown" had been stripped away, replaced by a name I didn't recognize. It was already registered in a neighboring county.

I felt the air leave the room, as if the very oxygen was being siphoned out of my lungs.

In a daze of rising panic, I right-clicked one of the documents to check the metadata. The author's name stared back at me, a ghost from a past I thought we had shared: *E. Simmons.* Emily's maiden name. She wasn't just building a business; she was reclaiming a version of herself that didn't include me.

My heart pounded against my ribs like a trapped bird as I scrolled through the staff bios. Two of our best instructors were listed as the "Founding Faculty." These were the same women who had stopped returning my calls two weeks ago, claiming they were "busy with family."

The betrayal wasn't loud. It didn't scream or slam doors or shatter glass. It was a silent frost that had moved in under the cover of night, killing the roots while the leaves were still green. It whispered behind closed blinds.

I sat back, my hands trembling so violently I had to tuck them under my thighs. For several minutes, the world went silent. I said nothing. I thought nothing. I simply let the weight of the truth settle into my bones like lead.

Emily had been building a new home while she was still living in mine. She had been taking the seeds from our harvest to plant a secret garden where I wasn't invited. There had been no fight. No warning. No honest conversation about needing to part ways. Just... duplicity.

I slowly closed the laptop, the click sounding like a finality I wasn't ready to face. I unplugged the flash drive and stared out the window. Outside, a neighbor's wind chimes danced in a sudden, sharp breeze, singing a hollow song.

Inside, a storm was forming in the center of my soul. And for the first time in my life, I wasn't sure if my roots were deep enough to weather it.

CHAPTER 7

THE CONFRONTATION

It was a Thursday, the kind of day where the air feels heavy and still, like the world is holding its breath before a Great Storm.

Classes had ended early, and the vibrant hum of students—the very lifeblood of this building—had faded into a haunting silence. The late-afternoon sun poured through the office windows, spilling across the room like liquid gold and casting long, skeletal shadows on the hardwood floors. It was the kind of evening that used to end with music, shared laughter, and perhaps a glass of wine between two women who once believed their dreams were grafted from the same vine. But not today. Today, the garden was silent.

I stood in the kitchen of the school's staff lounge, the printouts trembling in my hands like dry leaves in a winter wind. I had printed them that morning—harsh, jagged evidence of a life I didn't recognize. Website screenshots, staff listings, and a side-by-side comparison of our curriculum and BrightSmile's. The words were identical, a mirror image of the heart I had poured into this legacy.

I had read them at least ten times, praying for a different interpretation, seeking a way to see this as anything other than a harvest stolen. I had hoped I had misunderstood.

I hadn't.

The office door creaked open behind me, the sound echoing like a snap of a branch. Emily stepped in, her keys jingling in her hand—a domestic, familiar sound that now felt like a serrated edge. Her phone was tucked between her shoulder and ear, her voice light and unburdened.

I didn't move. I kept my back to her, a wall of silent grief.

Emily paused when she saw me, the casual rhythm of her day faltering. "Hey," she said, slipping the phone into her bag with a practiced ease. "Didn't know you were still here. I thought you'd gone to the gym."

I held the papers tighter, the edges biting into my palms. "We need to talk," I said. My voice was measured, a steady anchor in a rising tide of pain.

Emily set her bag down on the counter, her expression shifting into something guarded and unreadable. The "Sisterhood" was being replaced by "Strategy." "Okay?"

I slowly turned to face her. My eyes were filled with something far deeper than the heat of anger; they were filled with the cold, gray ash of mourning. I held out the papers.

"I found the flash drive, Emily. I saw the site. BrightSmile. I saw the curriculum—our curriculum—rebranded and stripped of its name. I saw our instructors listed under your banner."

Emily didn't speak right away. She didn't deny it. She simply inhaled slowly and leaned against the laminate counter, looking suddenly very tired. I continued, my voice soft but infused with the strength of a woman who knows her worth. "Why, Emily? Why did you plant a secret garden in the middle of our field? Why didn't you tell me?"

Emily looked away, her gaze fixing on the shadows lengthening on the floor. "I wasn wasn't trying to hide it forever, Crystal."

My jaw tightened, the "Mama Crown" in me rising to defend the integrity of our house. "But you were trying to hide it for now? While you sat at my table? While we prayed over these halls?"

A long, suffocating pause followed.

Emily crossed her arms, a defensive barrier. "I needed something that was mine. You have the money. You have the 'Mama Crown' voice. You're the one everyone looks to. I... I needed space to create something with my own name on it. Something where I wasn't just the shadow behind the light."

I blinked, the words stinging like salt in an open wound. "Your name was on everything here, Emily. We were the roots and the branches together. From the first napkin sketches to the final lesson plans, I never treated this like it was mine alone. I thought we were one organism."

"You were always the face," Emily muttered, her eyes lowered as if searching the floor for an exit. "I was just the one doing the grunt work. The teaching. The heavy lifting of the curriculum. You got the interviews, the praise, the awards. I got the admin load and the silent labor."

"That's not fair," I replied, my heart breaking for the version of the story she had told herself to justify the theft. "You chose the classroom because you loved the students. I took the parts you didn't want—the permits, the marketing, the midnight accounting—and I made them work so you *could* teach. I thought we were honoring each other's gifts."

Emily shook her head, her posture hardening. "I didn't want to fight. I didn't want to ask for more and be told no. I didn't want to feel like a beggar in a house I helped build."

"So instead, you left without leaving." My voice broke slightly, the weight of the betrayal finally fracturing my composure. "You stayed just long enough to use our soil to grow your own crop behind my back."

There was a long silence between us, thick with years of history, shared secrets, and the heavy scent of a dying season.

"I would've helped you," I whispered, the truth of it hanging in the air like a final prayer. "You know my heart, Emily. I would've invested in your dream just like you helped build mine. We could have expanded. We could have bloomed in two places. You didn't have to lie."

Emily looked up, her expression strained, the guilt flickering in her eyes before being replaced by a cold resolve. "I didn't lie, Crystal. I just... didn't tell you."

I let out a soft, pained laugh—a sound of pure disillusionment. "In the eyes of the Lord, Emily, and in the heart of a friend, it's the same thing. Silence is just a lie that hasn't been spoken yet."

Another silence followed. This one felt final, like the heavy thud of a tombstone settling into place.

Emily grabbed her bag slowly, her movements robotic. "I'll be gone by Monday. I won't cause a scene. I'll resign quietly. I'll send a formal letter for the board."

I didn't stop her. I didn't ask her to stay. I knew that once the root is severed, the branch cannot be taped back on and expected to live.

As Emily walked past, she paused at the doorway, the golden light silhouetting her one last time. "I never meant to hurt you, Crystal."

I didn't look up. I stayed staring at the floor, at the place where our shadows had once overlapped. "But you did. You took the crown and used it to cut me."

The door closed softly behind her, the click of the latch sounding like the final page of a long, beautiful chapter being torn out.

And just like that, the legacy we had built—the sisterhood I thought was eternal—cracked in half, leaving me standing in the ruins of a garden I no longer recognized.

CHAPTER 8

TORN ROOTS

Monday arrived, not with a bang, but with a hollow echo that reverberated through the very foundation of Crown Point Academy. Emily didn't return.

She didn't come in to collect the remains of her desk or offer a final word to the women who had looked up to her. There was no email of farewell to the staff, no handwritten letter left on the breakroom table, no closure to tie the loose ends of our four-year history. She simply vanished, leaving behind an empty office that felt like a sudden clearing in a dense forest. On her desk sat a worn coffee mug with a faint ring of dried brown at the bottom, a forgotten scarf draped like a shed skin over her chair, and the lingering, ghostly scent of the lavender she used to wear. That scent usually reminded me of peace; now, it smelled like a lingering winter.

I sat in the front office long after the final bell had rung and the school day had ended. My elbows rested on the cold mahogany desk, my fingers laced together so tightly my knuckles turned the color of bone. The building was too quiet. It wasn't the peaceful stillness of a garden at rest; this was the kind of silence that hums with the heavy absence of someone who had once filled every corner with her vibrant bloom.

The news of the departure spread through the staff like a slow-moving fog. No one dared to ask the hard questions out loud, but I could feel their confusion pressing against me in the hallways. Whispers swirled like dry leaves near the copier, and I saw the furrowed brows of my team during our morning meetings—eyes searching mine for a truth I wasn't yet ready to speak. Even the students noticed the shift in the atmosphere.

"She's not coming back, is she, Mama Crown?" one of the girls asked softly, leaning against the doorframe of the lobby.

I forced a smile, though it felt like a brittle mask. "She's moved on to a new season, honey. To new things."

I hoped my voice sounded like a blessing, but my eyes betrayed the mourning in my heart.

That week, I attempted to bury my grief in the soil of labor. I doubled my hours, trying to fill the void Emily had left behind. I taught her classes until my throat was dry, handled the surge of new enrollments, met with skeptical vendors, and responded to a mountain of emails at two in the morning. I restocked the supply closets with my own hands, finding a strange, numbing comfort in the physical work. Every night, I went home and collapsed on the couch, my body aching, only to rise before the sun and do it all again.

I didn't cry. I told myself that the gardener doesn't have time to weep when the harvest is at stake.

Not yet.

It wasn't until late Thursday evening, while I was staying behind to organize the student file cabinet—a task Emily had always handled with such meticulous care—that the wall finally broke. I pulled out a faded manila folder from our founding year and found a document bearing both of our signatures. Tucked behind it was a photo we had taken outside this very building on our opening day.

We were both grinning, our faces covered in streaks of ivory paint and our hearts full of a fire that felt unquenchable. We were holding a crooked "Grand Opening" banner, the corners reinforced with silver duct tape that we had applied with such hope.

That was when the truth finally hit me, cutting through the calloused layers of my busy heart. This wasn't just about losing a business partner or a lead instructor.

I had lost a sister.

I sank to the floor of the small supply room, the cold linoleum biting through my slacks, and pressed the photo to my chest. The weight of the last four years came crashing down on me: the long nights fueled by cheap coffee, the terrifying risks we took when the bank said no, the shared meals on the floor of empty classrooms, and the whispered dreams of what we would become.

The betrayal wasn't violent. It hadn't come in a sudden storm of shouts or slamming doors. It had crept in slowly, like a parasite—through avoidance, through the widening distance, through plans made in the dark.

These were torn roots, not severed ones. And in my spirit, I realized that torn roots are often worse; when a branch is severed cleanly, you know where to heal, but when roots are torn, you don't see the true extent of the damage until the tree begins to lean.

For the first time in weeks, I let myself weep. It wasn't a loud, desperate wailing, but a quiet, steady stream of tears—a mourning for the "what could have been" and the "what used to be." I let the water of my grief soak into the parched ground of my soul.

When I finally stood up and wiped my face, I wasn't the same woman who had walked in that morning. I felt weaker in some places, the raw ache of the betrayal still tender, but I felt stronger in others. I was a woman who had weathered a storm no one saw coming, and yet, I was still standing.

I placed the photo back into the file, tucked it safely into the drawer, and whispered to the empty, lavender-scented room: "I didn't lose everything. The branch may be gone, but I still have the soil. And by the grace of God, I'll plant again."

CHAPTER 9

GHOST HALLWAYS

The hum of the overhead lights used to be drowned out by the vibrant canopy of laughter that once sheltered these halls. Now, that laughter had withered, leaving behind a fluorescent buzz that echoed like a haunting. I walked the corridors of Crown Point Academy slowly, my steps heavy with the weight of a woman surveying a battlefield after the smoke has cleared. I trailed one hand along the cool, eggshell-white wall, feeling the slight texture of the paint as if it might still hold the warmth of the conversations it once absorbed—vows of sisterhood, prayers for the future, and the quiet rustle of dreams taking flight.

I passed the empty classrooms, where rows of chairs sat like headstones in a quiet cemetery. They had once held the ambition of women who arrived with nothing but a notebook and a prayer, their eyes full of a purpose I helped ignite. Now, it all felt like a museum exhibit. Preserved, yet paused. Intact, but hollowed out at the marrow.

It had been three weeks since Emily walked out, but her presence still clung to the corners of the building like a persistent winter frost. In Room 2, the whiteboard still bore her handwriting in the top right corner: *"Quiz Friday."* No one had dared to erase it. It felt like a phantom limb—a reminder of a function that was no longer there, a part of our root system that had been ripped away, leaving a jagged hole in the dirt.

In the front lobby, the mail slot held a small stack of unopened envelopes addressed to both of us. I sorted through them with a quiet, practiced dignity, noting the familiar handwriting of former students. They were likely sending updates on their new jobs, writing to us before they knew the garden had been compromised. The enrollment list for the next term sat on the counter, the numbers down by half—a thinning harvest that spoke of the drought to come.

Some students had left without a word, their seats suddenly vacant like fallen leaves. Others had followed the scent of a different bloom, transferring to BrightSmile—Emily's new program. I didn't harbor a drop of bitterness toward them. They didn't owe me their loyalty; they were simply chasing the light of opportunity, unaware that the light they followed had been stolen from the very lamp we lit together.

I stepped into Classroom 4. It had always been the sanctuary of my spirit. In the late afternoon, the sun poured through the west-facing windows in a defiant, golden flood. I used to sit here in the quiet after hours while Emily's voice drifted from her lecture across the hall. Back then, we were both lost in a shared purpose, our roots intertwined so deeply I thought we were one tree.

I sat in the teacher's chair now, my hands resting in my lap like two tired birds. I stared at the corkboard behind the desk, where a single photo remained pinned in the corner. It was a snapshot of a graduate named Lyla hugging both of us on the graduation stage. Her cap was tilted to the side, and her smile held enough joy to power the whole city.

"This place mattered," I whispered, my voice a small, flickering flame in the vast quiet.

The silence didn't argue. It simply settled around me, heavy and expectant.

I rose slowly, my joints aching with a fatigue that sleep couldn't touch, and walked toward the front of the building. The reception desk was tidier than usual—I had been organizing and scrubbing to keep my hands from shaking and my mind from wandering into the "why." Near the edge sat a framed certificate, its gold seal catching the fading light: *Women in the Workforce: Pioneers in Education, 2022.*

I ran my thumb across the glass, watching my reflection warp and shift in the surface. I looked like a woman wearing a crown that had grown too heavy to carry. Then, without warning, I took the frame off the counter and held it against my chest, feeling the hard edges of our success press into my heart.

I didn't cry this time. The season of weeping had passed, replaced by a cold, crystalline clarity. I just stood still, breathing deeply, letting the ache pass through me like a wave over a rock. I was the rock.

I turned and walked back to my office, placing the award gently in the back of a desk drawer. I knew I was standing at a crossroads. I had to choose: do I keep the school going with a fractured identity, trying to force a bloom from a broken branch, or do I let it go gracefully, allowing the soil to rest before I plant something new?

I didn't have the answer yet. The "Calm Mentor" in me was still waiting for the Spirit to move.

But as I reached for the light switch, I knew one thing with the certainty of the rising sun: I wouldn't let the silence be the last voice this building ever heard.

CHAPTER 10

THE LETTER SHE NEVER SENT

It started with one sentence, a single sprout of truth pushing through the heavy, frozen ground of my heart:

"I don't hate you."

I stared at the blinking cursor on my laptop, its rhythmic pulse like a steady heartbeat in the silence. The cool glow of the screen illuminated my face—tired, etched with the weariness of a woman who had been tilling a lonely field—in the dim sanctuary of my office. It was Saturday night. The school was still. I hadn't turned on the overhead lights; I preferred the soft desk lamp that cast a warm circle of gold over my keyboard, a small island of light in a sea of shadows.

I hadn't planned to write. But the words had lived inside me for weeks, pressing against my chest like steam under a lid, or like a seed that had grown too large for its shell and was desperate to break toward the surface.

So, I typed.

Emily, I don't hate you. I want to start there because the whispers in the street and the rumors in the halls probably say otherwise. They'll tell you I'm angry. They'll say I'm bitter, or maybe even jealous of the new garden you're trying to plant. I'm none of those things. I'm just sad. I'm mourning the shade we used to share.

I paused, exhaled a breath I felt I'd been holding since the day I found the flash drive, and kept going.

I opened my home to you when you were weathering your own winter. I let your children eat at my table like they were branches of my own tree. We dreamt this together, Emily. You held the paintbrush while I hammered the nails. You built the lessons—the beautiful, flowering curriculum—and I built the foundation, the deep roots that kept us steady in the wind. I never wanted to be a queen above you. I only wanted to wear a crown that matched yours as we stood side by side. Always. But somewhere along the way, you stopped standing with me. You started digging in a different direction.

I sat back, my fingers hovering over the keys, trembling slightly. The next part was the jagged stone in my throat.

You made a new school without me. You took our blueprint—the very DNA of our loyalty—and redrew it under a new name. That's your right. We all have the freedom to plant where we choose. But you never said goodbye. You just... left. Like I was a season you'd outgrown, or a soil that was no longer rich enough for your ambitions.

I blinked hard, swallowing the tight knot rising in my throat. I thought of the scripture about the fruit of the spirit, wondering how to find peace when the harvest felt stolen.

I've asked myself a hundred times what I missed. What signs were there in the dirt that I chose not to see? I still don't have an answer. But I do know this: I would have helped you. I would have invested in your dream with the same strength I used to build mine. You didn't have to go behind my back. You didn't have to behave like a thief in a garden you helped grow. You could've just asked me to walk with you in a new direction.

Instead, you chose to walk away in a silence that speaks louder than any shout.

I stopped. My hands were shaking now, not from weakness, but from the sheer force of letting go.

For twenty minutes, I read the letter back to myself. Every word rang with a truth that tasted like salt—honest, raw, and stinging with the beauty of a wound finally being cleaned. I imagined what Emily might say if she received it. Would she apologize? Would she justify her duplicity with more excuses? Would she simply ignore it?

As the "Calm Mentor" within me took a deep breath, I realized it didn't matter. This letter wasn't a bridge to Emily. It was a shovel for my own soul.

This letter wasn't for her. It was for me.

I highlighted the entire message, the blue block of text looking like a calm pool of water, and moved my cursor to the print icon. The old office printer whirred to life, a mechanical groan in the quiet room, spitting out the page slowly, as if it understood the weight of the confession it held. I took the warm paper, folded it once, then again, and walked to the back of the building.

In the rear parking lot sat the small metal fire pit we had used during staff retreats—nights where we had sat around the flames, laughing about the future. I placed the letter inside the cold iron belly of the pit. I struck a match, the sulfurous scent biting the air, and watched the tiny flame catch the corner of the page.

The fire curled the edges of the paper, turning the white to black and the ink to ash. I watched the words—the pain, the "why," the memories—turn into ribbons of smoke that drifted upward toward the stars. There is a holy cleansing in fire; it burns away the dead wood so the new growth has room to breathe.

I stood there until the paper was nothing but glowing embers, the heat warming my face. In the stillness of the Saturday night, I whispered to the wind:

"You don't owe me an apology. I forgive you anyway. I'm taking my crown back from the fire."

Then I turned, walked back inside the school that still felt like mine, and locked the door behind me with a firm, decisive click. The season of looking back was over.

CHAPTER II

THE LAST CEREMONY

The folding chairs had been cleaned and aligned in perfect, solemn rows, like seedlings waiting for the final sunrise of the season. Each one held a program printed on heavy linen paper, the edges crisp and folded just right. The school logo—a gold crown resting against an ivory shield—was centered at the top, shining with a quiet, defiant dignity. Beneath it, in looping, elegant script, the words read:

Crown Point Academy – Class of 2025

"More Than a Certificate—A Calling."

I stood at the front of the small room, the "Calm Mentor" in me adjusting my posture one last time. I wore a navy blue dress and the heels I hadn't put on since that hopeful Chamber of Commerce banquet years ago. My hair was curled at the ends, bouncing slightly as I moved, and I wore no makeup except for a thin layer of mascara—the waterproof kind, the kind that wouldn't run if my eyes decided to betray the stoic peace I had fought so hard to find.

It was the last graduation. The final harvest before the wintering of the school began.

I was closing the doors, but as I looked around the room, I knew it wasn't an act of defeat. Not because I had failed. But because the Spirit had whispered that the season was over. The soil of this particular field had given all it could to these specific roots, and it was time to let the land rest. Enrollment had dropped like falling leaves in autumn. My staff had moved on to their own new gardens, departing quietly and with my blessing. The community had shifted toward other programs, and I... I had no desire to fight a war for a territory that no longer fed my soul. Still, this night—this final group of graduates—deserved every ounce of my heart.

They entered the room one by one, their black gowns swishing with a sound like wind through wheat, shimmering under the hum of the fluorescent lights. Some came alone, heads held high with a new kind of pride. Some brought small, boisterous cheering squads. One girl, only nineteen years old, carried her infant son. He babbled and cooed throughout my opening speech, a sweet, living reminder that life continues even when institutions end.

I smiled through all of it, my heart swelling with a bittersweet joy.

When it came time for me to speak, I didn't bring a script. I didn't need one. I stood behind the wooden podium, looking out at the sea of hopeful, beautiful faces, and spoke from the deep, pulsing place in my chest that still believed in miracles.

"This school was built on love," I began, my voice steady as an anchor. "It was built on a whispered prayer, a tax ID number, and two friends who had no blueprint—just a shared heart and a willingness to get our hands dirty in the muck of life. Some of those dreams shifted. Some people we loved chose to plant elsewhere. But what remained in this soil was purpose. You are that purpose."

I looked at a woman in the front row and leaned in. "Every missed bus you caught up with. Every quiz you failed only to show up the next morning ready to try again. Every babysitter who canceled, leaving you to come to class with your baby on your hip because you knew your crown was worth the struggle... that is why this matters."

I paused, my voice growing thick, but I refused to let it break. "We didn't just give you technical training. You taught us how to rise. You taught us how to show up when the world told you to stay hidden. You taught us how to believe in the bloom again. Thank you for letting me be part of your root system."

The applause that followed was thunderous—not the polite, rhythmic clapping of a courtesy, but a roar of genuine connection. It was a sound of gratitude, a collective farewell. I handed out the certificates one by one, feeling the heat of their palms and the trembling of their fingers. For each student, I whispered a personal word, a seed for them to carry home.

"Don't let the ghosts of your past define your future."
"You are far more than the room you walked in from."
"This is not an ending, but a transplanting. Go and grow."

The final graduate was Tameka, a mother of four who had walked through the fire of losing her husband during her second year of study. She clutched her certificate to her chest and broke into quiet, heaving sobs. I didn't just hand her a paper; I pulled her in and hugged her. Tight. Long. The way sisters do when they know the cost of the journey.

After the ceremony, the lights dimmed. The families filtered out into the night, their laughter fading into the parking lot. The students snapped their final photos by the school logo, capturing the gold crown one last time.

I stayed behind.

I walked into each empty classroom, my heels clicking against the floor like a heartbeat. I turned off the lights, room by room, whispering a soft "thank you" and a "goodbye" to every corner that had witnessed a breakthrough. In the front office, I paused at my desk. It still held the gold nameplate: *Crystal Jameson – Director.*

I picked it up, feeling the cool metal and the weight of the title. I held it for a long while, reflecting on the woman who had started this journey in a diner booth with a lottery ticket. Then, I slipped it into my purse.

"You're coming with me," I whispered to the nameplate, or perhaps to the woman I had become.

Outside, the moon was full and bright, lighting the parking lot like a silver stage. I turned one last time to look at the building—the one we had painted with our own hands, the one we had prayed over until the walls felt holy, the one we had fought for until our hearts were weary.

And for the first time in months, I didn't feel the cold grip of grief. I felt the warm, expansive grace of release. The crown wasn't the building. The crown was the strength I carried inside as I walked away.

CHAPTER 12

DRIFT AND DISCOVERY

There was no party. There was no grand send-off with speeches and wilted flower arrangements.

I left quietly, slipping away before the morning sun could fully wake the town. I packed only two suitcases: one for the essentials of the body, and one for the healing of the soul. In that second bag were the things no one else would've thought to carry—my most intimate journal, a faded copy of my very first school brochure, my son's heavy college hoodie, and a single, cream-colored envelope with the words "Start Again" written across the front in my own steady hand. I didn't know exactly where the wind was blowing me. I only knew that the soil here had become too saturated with memory; I had to find a place where I could breathe until my own roots felt strong again.

My first stop was Italy. Venice, to be exact.

I spent days sitting on the stone steps of buildings that had stood for centuries, watching the gondolas drift under ancient bridges as if time itself had decided to pause and rest. Tourists snapped photos of the surface, but I found myself looking at the water—how it moved, how it yielded, how it held everything up without breaking. I sat in small cafes, drinking cappuccinos that warmed my palms, letting my thoughts unravel like a length of old, silk ribbon. No one there knew my name. No one asked what I did for a living or how many buildings I had raised from the dirt. I was anonymous—and in that anonymity, I found a terrifying, beautiful freedom.

I opened my journal one afternoon near the Grand Canal and wrote:

"I spent so much time building a canopy for others to hide under that I forgot who I was when I wasn't the one holding up the sky. I am learning that even a tree must shed its leaves to survive the winter."

From the canals of Italy, I followed a calling to Kenya.

I volunteered at a women's co-op, teaching basic business skills and designing flyers for a local market. The women there wore headwraps in colors so vibrant they looked like a garden in permanent bloom. They laughed with their whole bodies, a deep, resonant sound that seemed to come from the earth itself. They didn't know what Crown Point Academy was. They didn't care about my past betrayals. But they knew purpose.

One woman, Miriam, pulled me aside one afternoon under the shade of a wide acacia tree. She spoke through a translator, her eyes holding a depth that made me feel seen in a way I hadn't felt in years. "You look like someone who knows the weight of loss," she said softly. "But you carry your pain like a gift bag—quiet, but full of something the rest of us need."

I couldn't find the words to respond. I simply reached out and hugged her, feeling the strength in her arms—the strength of a woman who had also survived the fire.

In the evenings, I would sit beneath the African sky, which stretched wide and endless above me like the very palm of God. The stars blanketed the horizon like scattered dreams waiting to be reclaimed. In that vastness, the "Mama Crown" in me began to stir again. I realized I could be whole. Not the same—never the same—but whole. My roots were finding water in new soil.

From Kenya, I traveled back west to Northern California.

My son, Deon, had recovered his strength. He was training with a European league team now, his spirit restored after the season of sickness that had nearly uprooted us all. He had flown home to a quiet corner of Napa Valley to rest and reset before the next climb. We met there—just the two of us. No press, no scouts, no distractions.

We sat at a small table overlooking a vineyard where the vines were heavy with fruit. Over dinner, he reached across the table and held my hand, his grip firm and familiar.

"You didn't tell me about all of it, Mom," he said, his voice dropping an octave. "Emily. The school. How it all ended in the dark."

I smiled faintly, looking out at the rows of grapes. "Because I didn't want you to carry my heartbreak on top of your own. You had your own race to run, Deon."

He squeezed my hand, his eyes shining with a maturity that proved he was my greatest harvest. "I would've carried it. You've carried me my whole life. You don't have to protect the crown alone anymore."

We sat in silence for a long time—the good kind of silence that doesn't need to be filled with explanations. He had grown into everything I had dreamed of: strong, thoughtful, resilient. He was a man who understood that true crowns aren't made of gold and ego. They're shaped by sacrifice and polished by the tears we shed for others.

I stayed another week in the valley, breathing in the crisp California air and letting my mind rest from the constant labor of planning, fixing, and solving. I hiked trails that smelled of eucalyptus and damp earth, picked wild lavender, and walked barefoot across the cool, smooth stones of a hidden river.

On my final day, I found my way to a small, sun-drenched tattoo studio on a quiet street in Santa Rosa. The artist was a woman with long, silver locs and a smile that felt like a blessing.

"What are we putting on you today, sister?" she asked, her voice like a song.

I pulled a small, crumpled slip of paper from my pocket—the one I had been carrying since Italy—and handed it over. It read: *Forgive what tried to break you. Then rise taller.*

The artist nodded slowly, a look of recognition passing between us. "Where do you want it?"

I touched my ribcage, right over the place where the breath often caught when I thought of the betrayal. "Here," I said. "Right here. Where it hurt the most."

I winced as the needle began its rhythmic buzz, but I smiled through the sharp sting. I felt the ink settling into my skin, marking the end of one journey and the beginning of another. I wasn't just surviving the storm anymore; I was becoming the sky. I was writing a new story now—not just in ink, but in the holy intention of a woman who finally knew her own worth.

CHAPTER 13

PLANTING NEW SEEDS

The air smelled different in Virginia.

It was crisper, more honest—like the world had been scrubbed clean by a persistent, holy rain. Perhaps it was just the clarity I carried within me, the stillness that follows months of restless motion, the certainty that only arrives after a season of absolute unraveling. I chose a small town nestled between rolling hills that looked like the earth was breathing in deep, green swells. There were no chain stores to crowd the horizon, just one post office, a single traffic light, and a community where folks waved from their porches without needing to know your name before they offered a smile.

I rented a modest brick storefront on the corner of Main Street. It had been a bakery once, decades ago. Even now, the faded, sweet scent of cinnamon and yeast still lingered in the cracks of the old floorboards, a ghost of past nourishment.

The windows were thick with the dust of abandonment, covered in yellowed flyers from two years ago. I spent my first full day there scrubbing the glass until my arms ached and my palms were raw. I watched as the grime gave way, allowing the morning light to pour in freely—unbothered, beautiful, and searching. It felt like I was clearing the cataracts from my own vision, finally seeing the path God had laid out for me in the quiet.

There was no grand announcement this time. No polished ribbon-cutting ceremony with local dignitaries. Most importantly, there was no co-founder standing in my shadow, clutching a secret plan. It was just me, the silence, and a dream that had been refined in the fire until only the gold remained.

I named it **Crown & Root**.

"Because a crown without roots," I told the landlord as I handed him the first month's deposit, my voice steady with a new kind of authority, "has no legacy. It's just a heavy hat waiting to fall. But a tree with deep roots? It can survive any storm and still reach for the sky."

The town took to me slowly, cautiously, as small towns often do with "transplanted" souls. But when word spread that I was opening a new kind of school—one that would teach the technical precision of dental technology, yes, but also the vital skills of life, confidence, and the grit of entrepreneurship—curiosity turned to a warm, simmering excitement.

I painted the walls myself, refusing to hire out the labor. I needed to feel the transformation in my own grip.

I chose warm earth tones—deep sienna and moss—with bold, royal purple accent walls and fixtures of brushed gold. Each long, deliberate brushstroke felt like I was reclaiming something stolen: my joy, my vision, my right to lead. As the colors deepened, I felt my own spirit darkening into something more resilient, less easily bruised by the world.

I built the curriculum at the small kitchen table of my rental house during the blue hours of the night and the amber hours of the dawn. I sat with my Bible on one side and my business journals on the other. I created modules that asked the hard, introspective questions most programs never dared to touch:

"Who were you before the world told you who to be?"
"What does success mean when the applause dies down and no one is watching?"
"How do you protect the peace of your inner sanctum in a room that doesn't value your presence?"

It wasn't just a school anymore. It was a sanctuary. It was healing disguised as education, a place where the broken could come to be grafted into something stronger.

I ordered a hand-carved wooden sign to hang above the front door. It was heavy, solid oak that smelled of the forest. It read:

Crown & Root Institute: Grow. Rise. Stay Grounded.

On the day the sign was finally installed, I stood across the street in the brilliant morning sun, my hands tucked into my pockets. I let the tears come then. They weren't the hot, stinging tears of the diner booth or the ragged sobs of the supply closet. They were a quiet, overflowing stream—a baptism of sorts.

I wasn't crying because I was sad. I was crying because for the first time in my life, I was building not from the desperate need of the "Mama Crown" to prove her worth, but from a place of quiet, unshakable power. I finally knew that while the fire may have scorched the branches, it only made the roots grow deeper.

CHAPTER 14

WHEN THE CROWN FITS AGAIN

The halls of Crown & Root weren't wide; they were intimate, like the corridors of a heart that has finally learned to open again. The classrooms weren't lined with the sterile glare of brand-new technology or the cold perfection of polished tile. There were no automated attendance systems to categorize souls, no digital smartboards to replace human connection. But there was life—raw, vibrant, and unyielding.

The hum of second chances echoed through every wall, vibrating in the very floorboards like a low, steady prayer.

Students came early—some still in their faded scrubs from grueling overnight shifts, the scent of hospital soap and exhaustion clinging to them. Others arrived late but breathless and apologetic, children in tow like small, curious fruit, or shadows under their eyes from the weight of trying to make life work. I never shamed them. I welcomed every one of them by name, looking them in the eye until they remembered they were seen.

I had always believed that true education should make room for real people—the bruised, the busy, the brave—not just the perfect ones. Within three months, the soil was so fertile that our enrollment doubled.

Word spread quickly through the nearby towns, a quiet wildfire of hope. It wasn't because of a flashy marketing campaign or a glossy brochure, but because my students went home and whispered to their families, their cousins, and their coworkers: "She listens." "She believes in the seeds we carry." "She teaches what actually matters."

I added night classes—one specifically for mothers and another for students re-entering the workforce after incarceration, souls who had spent too long in the shade and were ready for the sun. The school buzzed with laughter, purpose, and the kind of fierce determination that didn't care about the shallow metrics of appearances. We were building a canopy together.

I started each week with a message scrawled on the whiteboard in the lobby, a simple affirmation for the journey: *"You are not behind. You are not too late. You are right on time."*

One afternoon, while I was clearing the digital clutter of my inbox, I found a letter. It was from a student I didn't immediately recall enrolling—a quiet girl named Denisha who rarely spoke in class, a sapling who stayed in the back, observing the world. The note read:

Ms. Crystal, I know you don't know me well. I sit in the back. I don't raise my hand much because I've been taught to be small. But I need you to know something. I read your story online. I saw that old article—the one about what happened to you, your old school, and the friend who left. And I didn't feel sorry for you. I felt seen. Because I've been used too. I've had people pretend to love me only to uproot me when it was convenient for them. But you didn't let that fire stop you. You built again, and you built better. And now I believe I can too. I'm graduating next week, and I'm standing tall. Because of you. Thank you.

I read it twice. Then three times.□

By the fourth time, my hands trembled.□

It wasn't because I was broken or because the old wounds were reopening. It was because I was finally, fully healing. My roots had finally reached the deep water.

I printed the letter and pinned it directly above my desk. It wasn't a trophy of what I had survived, but a compass pointing toward who I had become because of the fire.

The crown no longer sat on a shelf in a dark room, waiting to be polished or reclaimed from a thief. I didn't wear it out of a desperate need for pride or to prove a point to those who had walked away.

I didn't need to wear it at all.

I was the crown. My life was the fruit.□

And this time, the fit was perfect.

CHAPTER 15

LETTERS OF RECOMMENDATION

The cool, medicinal scent of eucalyptus lingered in the air—I had started burning essential oils in the afternoons, a fragrant shield meant to help my students find a center of calm during the storm of finals week. My office window was cracked just enough to invite the Virginia breeze to dance with the curtains, while a soft gospel playlist hummed like a low, rhythmic prayer beneath the staccato click of keyboards and the distant, familiar chatter from the hallways.

It was nearly graduation. The season of harvest was upon us once again.

I sat at my desk with a stack of manila folders, their edges softened by the heat of my hands. Each one held a student's life in paper form: transcripts, test scores, attendance records, and the neon sticky tabs where I'd scribbled notes throughout the semester. These weren't just data points to me; they were the measurements of new growth. What mattered most, however, were the letters I was currently drafting—recommendations for job placements, apprenticeships, and certifications.

This wasn't a chore to be checked off a list. To me, this was sacred work—the act of tilling the ground for someone else's success.

Each letter was a mirror, reflecting the person I saw blooming beneath the sterile facts of a resume. I didn't write with the detached, clinical ink of an administrator. I wrote as a woman who had walked every thorny hallway of struggle my students were now trying to leave behind. I knew the weight of the dirt they were climbing out of, and I knew how to describe the strength of the roots they had developed in the dark.

I paused over one file: Jameela Harris.

A single mother and former foster youth, Jameela had arrived at our doors with her head bowed and her spirit guarded. She had failed two midterms early in the semester, her confidence wilting under the heat of the pressure. But she had stayed after every class, her jaw set with a determination that reminded me of my own early days in the diner booth. She once told me, in a rare moment of vulnerability that cracked open her tough exterior, that this program was the first thing she'd ever dared to finish. She was terrified of her own potential to rise.

I smiled, the memory warming my chest, and began to type.

To Whom It May Concern, I am honored to recommend Jameela Harris—a woman of unmatched perseverance and a quiet, subterranean brilliance. Her transcripts will show a steady climb toward the light. But her character? That is a crown you will only truly understand when you meet her. She does not just work; she overcomes...

I read it back and nodded. This was my favorite part of the labor. Not the grading, not the grueling board meetings, or the dry compliance reports. This. Advocating. Believing. Using my voice to speak someone else's name into rooms they weren't yet invited to enter.

The door creaked open, breaking my focus. It was Ms. Lorraine, my receptionist and a former student who had grown into a formidable branch of this school. She held two more folders, a knowing, weary grin on her face.

"Two more for you," she said, setting them on the corner of my desk. "I told them you'd do it. They said they didn't want to bother the Director."

I chuckled, reaching for the new files. "It's not a bother, Lorraine. It's a legacy. We're just making sure the roots are deep enough to hold the weight of their futures."

Lorraine lingered at the door for a moment, her expression softening into something deep and reflective.

"You know, they don't just need your signatures and your letters," she said gently. "They need your story. A lot of these women are here because someone whispered to them about what you overcame to build this place. They don't just see a school director, Crystal. They see proof that the fire doesn't have to be the end of the forest."

I felt a familiar, tight knot form in my throat, a mix of humility and the lingering weight of my own past.

"I'm not sure I ever intended to be proof of anything," I replied.

"Well," Lorraine said softly, "sometimes the crown gets heavy because it's carrying everyone else's hope, too. But it looks good on you."

She left me then, and I sat in the silence for a long moment, the eucalyptus and the gospel music wrapping around me like a familiar blanket. I returned to the keyboard, my fingers finding their rhythm.

One letter after another.□

One open door after another.

With every word I typed, I was reminded of a simple, beautiful truth: my story hadn't ended with the cold ash of betrayal. It had expanded into a bridge—long, sturdy, and wide. And my students were finally crossing it, walking out of the shadows and toward the sun.

CHAPTER 16
FINAL WALKTHROUGH

The keys jingled in her hand—a metallic song of endings and beginnings—as Crystal stood alone at the entrance of Crown Point Academy. This was not the new sanctuary she had built in Virginia, the resilient "Crown & Root," but the original site of her first bloom and her deepest pruning.

She had driven back for one final walkthrough before the building was turned over to the local college that had purchased it. The deed had been finalized months ago, and the college promised to continue community education in its halls, planting their own dreams in the soil she had tilled. But Crystal needed to see it one last time—on her own terms. She needed to walk through the shadows to ensure she was truly ready for the light.

The security code still worked, the buttons familiar beneath her fingertips. The door clicked open with the same high-pitched chime it always had. For a heartbeat, she expected to hear the ghosts of the past—Emily's sharp, rhythmic laughter, the bustling chatter of students carrying heavy textbooks, or the echo of her own voice offering affirmations in the hallway.

But it was silent. The air was still, heavy with the scent of floor wax and old paper.

Dust motes danced like tiny spirits in the sunbeams slicing through the window blinds, illuminating the stillness. The walls, once a vibrant ivory and gold, looked weary and faded now, as if they too were tired of holding up the weight of the stories told within them. The nameplate on her old office door had been removed, leaving only a faint, rectangular shadow on the wood—a scar where her identity used to hang for the world to see.

She walked the halls slowly, not rushing a single step. Her heels clicked against the linoleum, a solitary rhythm in the void.

In Room 2, she reached out and touched the glass where they had first installed the long mirrors. They had once been covered in motivational quotes written in bold dry-erase markers. One particular phrase, though long erased, seemed to shimmer on the surface: *"You are more than what broke you."* Crystal smiled. That quote had been the trellis that held her up during her darkest months of winter, a reminder that even when the branches are snapped, the root remains.

In Room 4, she sat in the teacher's chair, the very same one she had collapsed in, weeping, on the day Emily's betrayal was laid bare. This time, she wasn't crying. She was simply remembering. It was a gentle ache, like the memory of an old injury that only throbbed when the weather changed. It was no longer a fresh wound; it was a testimony.

In the hallway outside the staff lounge, she noticed something small tucked into the corner of the cork bulletin board—a single, stray photo of the first graduating class. She had thought she took them all down, but this one had stayed behind, a hidden seed. She pulled it gently from the pin and stared at the faces.

They were all smiling. Every single one of them.

She knew their stories—the single mothers, the survivors, the women who had been told they would never bloom. They weren't smiling because life had suddenly become perfect; they were smiling because, in that room, they had believed they could reclaim their own crowns. And they had.

Crystal folded the photo with practiced care and slipped it into her coat pocket, close to her heart.

Her final stop was the front office. Her desk was an empty island in the middle of the room. The drawers had been cleared of the pens, the ledgers, and the scattered dreams of the last few years. But taped inside the back of the top drawer, barely hanging on by a sliver of yellowed tape, was a handwritten note from one of her former instructors.

You taught us how to build, Crystal, but more importantly—you taught us how to keep building even when the world tries to tear us down. You showed us the strength of the root. Thank you.

She placed her hand over the ink, closed her eyes, and inhaled deeply, letting the grace of the words settle into her spirit.

Then, she stood.

She didn't take anything else—not a souvenir, not a chair, not a frame. She didn't need the physical remnants of a building to prove she had been there. She had her memory. She had her growth. She had her peace, which surpassed all understanding.

At the exit, she turned around one last time. The building was empty of furniture, but she didn't feel the hollow ache of loneliness. She felt honored. It was the kind of honor that doesn't come from gold-plated awards or the roar of applause—but from the quiet, holy satisfaction of finishing well.

She placed the keys in the lockbox, heard the click of the lid, and whispered under her breath: "Thank you for everything. You were the fire that refined me. You made me who I needed to become."

And with that, she walked toward her car, her head held high. She wasn't escaping a past she hated; she was stepping into a future she had earned. She was finally, truly free.

CHAPTER 17

HEADLINES AND HEARSAY

The first headline caught her off guard, a digital ghost rising from a grave she thought she had sealed.

It was a Google Alert set long ago—back when she was still a gardener of the first dream, trying to track every small sprout of press coverage for Crown Point Academy. She had forgotten to turn it off, and now it hummed in her pocket like a stinging nettle.

"Co-Founders of Crown Point Part Ways—New School Opens in Nearby County."

Crystal clicked the link out of curiosity more than anything else, but as the page loaded, she felt that familiar tightening in her chest, the old fire trying to lick at her peace.

It was a local digital blog. The article was short—barely three paragraphs—but the tone spoke volumes between the lines. It painted a picture of a clean, inevitable progression. It made it seem as though Emily had simply "evolved" into a higher calling, while Crystal had been the one "reluctant to change," a stubborn root refusing to let go of old soil.

There was no mention of the betrayal that had left the original garden in ruins. No hint that the curriculum had been duplicated, leaf for leaf and branch for branch. No credit given for the years of startup capital, the sleepless nights spent balancing ledgers, or the countless hand-printed flyers Crystal had distributed in the driving rain while others slept.

It was a smooth, clinical rewrite of history. To the world, it looked like a natural blooming. Only Crystal knew the branches had been stolen.

She closed the tab, her fingers trembling slightly as she set the phone on the desk.

Two days later, the notification chime rang again, sharper this time.

"BrightSmile: New Training School Run by Former Co-Founder Garners Early Praise."

The photo beneath the headline was professional and crisp—Emily, standing in a modern, sun-drenched classroom with her arms crossed. she was smiling with the confidence of someone who had nothing to regret, wearing a look of effortless victory.

Crystal stared at the screen for a long time, the blue light reflecting in her eyes. The "Mama Crown" in her felt a surge of righteous heat. She thought about calling the reporter. She thought about writing a public statement, a manifesto of the truth. She even opened her notes app and drafted a post that began:

"Since no one wants to tell the truth, let me tell you what it actually costs to build a legacy when loyalty is traded for a shortcut..."

But as her thumb hovered over the "post" button, she felt a shift—a quiet, cooling breeze in her spirit. She looked at the words. They were jagged. They were defensive. They were the sounds of someone trying to fix a crown that had already been replaced by something better.

She didn't post it. Instead, she powered down the phone, the screen going black and reflecting her own steady gaze.

She went for a walk.

Down the old gravel trail behind her Virginia rental, she moved through a path where the trees whispered in a language of endurance and the wind didn't ask for explanations or apologies. The air smelled of damp earth and pine—the scent of a forest that knew how to grow back after a fire.

Let them talk, she thought, the gravel crunching firmly beneath her feet.

Let them twist the narrative. Let them paint me as the one who was too slow, too soft, or too stuck in the old ways.

She realized she didn't need to clear her name in the court of public opinion. When you are rooted in the Truth, you don't have to shout to be heard. Because in private, in the quiet sanctuary of her own soul, she had a peace that the headlines could never touch.

At the next staff meeting at Crown & Root, she saw the reality that no blog could capture. She noticed how her students leaned in, their eyes wide and hungry, when she spoke about integrity. She saw how the new intern unconsciously mimicked her posture—head held high, shoulders back—when answering difficult questions. She watched as the local janitor brought his teenage niece to enroll, telling Crystal plainly, "I know she'll be safe with you. I know you'll teach her right."

Those moments didn't make headlines. There were no cameras for the quiet steadying of a young woman's heart. But they mattered more than a thousand "likes" or a front-page feature.

Later that night, Crystal pulled out her journal and let the ink flow like a prayer:

Let them underestimate the quiet growth. Let them call you forgotten while you are simply being refined. While they are chasing the loud, fleeting applause of men, choose to plant something deeper. Roots don't need credit to do their work. They don't need a headline to draw water. They just need time, and the faithfulness of the One who provides the rain.

She closed the journal and made a cup of herbal tea, the steam rising in a gentle curl. Outside her window, the small Virginia town slept peacefully under a blanket of stars.

In that stillness, she finally smiled. Because she knew the loudest truth isn't shouted in a digital feed.

It's lived in the fruit of the harvest.

CHAPTER 18

THE DRIVE SOUTH

She didn't tell anyone she was leaving.

There was no dramatic farewell, no final meeting to delegate tasks, and certainly no social media post to announce her absence. There was just her car, a full tank of gas, and the soft, internal decision that her spirit needed to stretch beyond the familiar edges of her daily routine. Her soul felt like a pot-bound plant—the roots circling inward, tight and suffocating—and it was time to transplant herself into the unknown.

It had been nearly five years since she had done anything spontaneous. For half a decade, every hour had been scheduled, every breath committed, every ounce of her energy promised to someone else's growth. But on this particular Thursday morning, Crystal woke up before the alarm could even think of ringing. She packed a single overnight bag with the essentials and a worn Bible, and she simply drove.

No map. No curated playlist. Just the vast, holy weight of silence.

The tires hummed against the pavement as the backroads of Virginia unfolded before her like a story she hadn't finished reading. She watched the world wake up through the windshield—cotton fields dusted with silver frost, rusted barns standing like stoic elders against the horizon, and roadside diners with neon signs that buzzed and flickered against the retreating morning fog.

Somewhere between Charlottesville and the North Carolina border, where the soil begins to turn that deep, honest shade of rust-red, she turned off her phone. No GPS to tell her where to turn. No pings to remind her of what she owed. No digital updates on anyone else's "blooming."

Just the sound of her own breath, steady and calm for the first time in a long season.

By midday, she found herself in a small town she'd never heard of—a place the world seemed to have tucked away for safekeeping. It was the kind of town with one gas station, one white-steepled church, and a single blinking light at the main intersection that seemed to suggest there was no reason to hurry. She pulled into a diner—white bricks, red awning, and the words "Homemade Biscuits" painted in flaking, optimistic letters on the window. Inside, the air was thick; it smelled like butter, woodsmoke, and history.

She chose a booth by the window, the vinyl seat cracking slightly under her weight, and ordered a sweet tea and a breakfast plate that reminded her of her grandmother's kitchen. The waitress—a woman with gray hair pulled into a tight, sensible bun and a name tag that read *Dorothy*—brought her food without the intrusion of small talk. She gave only a gentle nod and a knowing smile, as if she had served a thousand women on the same journey.

Crystal ate slowly, savoring the textures. She watched people pass outside the window like scenes in someone else's movie. She didn't know their names, their sorrows, or their triumphs. They didn't know her history or the weight of the crown she had been carrying. There was something sacred in that anonymity; it was a rest for the soil of her identity.

When the bill came, Dorothy lingered for a moment, wiping the table with a damp cloth.

"You look like you're running from something," the older woman said softly. Her voice wasn't prying; it was kind, seasoned by years of observation.

Crystal smiled, feeling the truth of it resonate in her chest. "Maybe. Or maybe I'm running toward something I forgot how to name."

Dorothy nodded as if the answer were a familiar scripture. "Well, honey... rest when you need. No one ever wins a race against themselves. The road will still be there when you're ready to walk it."

Crystal left a generous tip, folded her receipt into the back of her journal, and drove a little farther until she found a weather-worn bench at a quiet lakeside park. She sat there, the wood rough against her palms, until the sun began to dip behind the pines, painting the water with strokes of vibrant orange and deep lavender.

She closed her eyes, the cool air touching her face, and whispered into the dusk:

"I am not what was done to me. I am not the betrayal I had to survive. I am what I choose to build next, from the roots up."

That night, she checked into a roadside inn with scratchy towels and walls that held the peace of a thousand temporary stays. Before sleep took her, she sat on the edge of the bed and wrote in her journal:

Day 1. No answers yet. Just air.

Day 1. No pain tonight. Just a pause.

Day 1. I am still here. My roots are still reaching. And I am still becoming.

She fell asleep to the rhythmic sound of her own breathing, realizing for the first time that being "just Crystal" was finally, beautifully, enough.

CHAPTER 19

A Cottage in Virginia

I hadn't planned to stay. When the roots of your life have been ripped from the earth, you often feel as though you are meant to keep moving, a tumbleweed at the mercy of the wind. But sometimes, the Spirit leads you to a place where the soil is quiet enough for you to finally hear your own heartbeat.

I found the cottage online late one night, the blue light of the laptop reflecting in my weary eyes. It was a listing buried deep on a rental site, featuring grainy photos that looked like a faded memory, accompanied by a caption that spoke directly to my exhaustion: *"Peaceful getaway for thinkers and healers."*

It was nestled in the emerald foothills of western Virginia, a small sanctuary of wood and stone. It had chipped white paint that reminded me of a well-loved Bible cover, climbing ivy that hugged the porch rails like an old friend, and heavy-headed hydrangeas that bloomed in shades of periwinkle and lace, as if someone still tended to the place with a quiet, persistent love.

The landlord, Miss Lila—a retired librarian with silver curls and a voice that tinkled like windchimes in a gentle breeze—handed me the keys after a single phone call. She didn't ask for a resume or a mission statement; she simply listened to the silence between my words.

"You don't sound like someone looking for a vacation, dear," she had said softly, her wisdom reaching through the phone line. "You sound like someone looking for a place to be invisible and remembered all at once. A place to let the fallow ground rest."

I had driven there with my car still dusty from the long roads of my escape, my heart still cluttered with the jagged remnants of the past. The first night in the cottage, the silence was so absolute it felt like a weighted blanket. I slept for eleven hours—a deep, dreamless slumber that I hadn't known since before the school, before the betrayal, before the fire. No alarms screamed at me. No digital noise demanded my attention. No heavy obligations sat on my chest. There was just the stillness of the mountain air.

In the days that followed, I found myself rising with the sun, watching a congregation of birds gather at the feeder outside the kitchen window. I picked up habits I hadn't made time for in years—making tea in an actual copper kettle, listening for the whistle, and opening the windows wide to let the curtains dance. I started reading poetry again, letting the rhythm of the stanzas mend the frayed edges of my thoughts.

Every morning, I swept the porch. It was a simple, repetitive motion, the bristles of the broom scratching against the wood, helping me feel grounded in the physical world. The air here was a tonic—less heavy than the humid atmosphere of expectation I had left behind. It was thin and sweet, smelling of pine needles and damp earth.

The nearby town was small and hushed, a collection of brick storefronts and kind eyes. It was the kind of place where everyone knew your name within a week, but no one asked the invasive questions that usually followed a woman like me. The local bookstore owner began calling me "Miss Crystal" by my second visit, and the barista at the corner coffee shop had memorized my preference for extra honey by the third.

It didn't take long before the slow, steady rhythm of the cottage became a rhythm of true healing. For the first time in my life, I started to believe that the crown I carried wasn't something I had to build or earn through endless labor. I was beginning to see that my worth wasn't found in the height of the branches I grew for others to see, but in the quiet strength of the roots that grew in the dark, silent places of my soul. I was learning that I was enough, even when I wasn't building anything at all.

CHAPTER 20

THE QUILT AND THE QUESTION

On a Tuesday morning, a soft, rhythmic knock echoed against the heavy wood of the cottage door. Miss Lila stood on the porch, her silver curls catching the early light, holding a bundle of folded fabric that smelled faintly of cedar and forgotten summers.

"I was cleaning out the cedar chest in the attic," she said, her voice like the gentle chime of a bell, "and I found something that felt like it belonged to you. Some things don't want to be stored away; they want to be used."

Crystal took the bundle and unfolded the quilt gently across the back of the sofa. It was a heavy, hand-stitched labor of love, made from mismatched pieces of calico, worn denim, and scraps of floral silk—old clothing that had surely seen a lifetime of Sunday services and kitchen dances. Thick, cream-colored thread anchored the patches together. The pattern was jagged but beautiful—an intentional chaos that mirrored the complexity of a life well-lived. In the center, embroidered in delicate lilac thread that stood out against a patch of deep indigo, was a phrase that made the room go still:

"Every crown leaves roots."

Crystal's breath caught in her throat, a sharp intake of air that felt like a sudden frost. She stared at the words, her heart hammering a frantic rhythm against her ribs.

Miss Lila saw her reaction and reached out, her hand weathered and soft as parchment, resting briefly on Crystal's arm. She smiled with the wisdom of a woman who had seen many winters turn to spring. "I stitched that one when I finally retired from the library. I used to think crowns were only for royalty—for those born into gold and ease. Then I realized they were for survivors, too. For those who stayed upright when the wind tried to snap them. But a crown is heavy, dear. It only stays on the head if the roots go deep enough into the soul."

Crystal ran her fingers across the raised stitching of the lilac thread. *Every crown leaves roots.* The phrase stuck to her spirit like a burr all day, refuse to be shaken off.

She laid the quilt at the foot of her bed that night and stared at it for a long time by the light of a single candle. She didn't reach for it because she was cold; she reached for it because she needed the weight of what it represented. She needed to feel the truth that even broken, mismatched things—the scraps of a life torn apart by betrayal—could be stitched back together into something that could hold you through the night.

She realized then that crowns weren't always gleaming things worn for the world to applaud. Sometimes, they were carried quietly in the secret decisions to keep going, in the slow work of healing, and in the courageous act of choosing peace over the performance of success. The roots were the parts no one saw, the internal anchors that kept the crown from slipping when the earth shook.

The next morning, the sun rose with a clear, insistent light. Crystal pulled out her laptop for the first time in weeks, the silver lid feeling cold and unfamiliar beneath her palms.

She didn't open social media to see the headlines of "BrightSmile." She didn't check the frantic, unread emails from the life she had left behind. Instead, she opened a clean, white, blank document—a field of fresh snow—and typed one solitary sentence:

"If I built again, I'd build slower—and only from the bedrock of truth."

Then she sat back, took a deep, lung-filling breath of the mountain air, and let the idea take root in the quiet, fertile soil of her renewed mind.

CHAPTER 21

RETURNING TO SELF

Crystal began returning to herself the way someone returns to an old house—gently, room by room, cleaning out what no longer fits and making space for what always did. It was a slow tilling of the inner soil, pulling up the weeds of other people's expectations to see what original seeds still lived in the dark.

She stopped wearing makeup for a while. Not because she was hiding, but because she no longer felt the need to perform for a world that only valued the bloom and ignored the root. Her skin felt like it belonged to her again—cool, honest, and unmasked. She looked in the mirror and didn't see the "Mama Crown" the public demanded; she saw Crystal, a woman whose beauty was no longer a shield, but a quiet, steady light.

She cut her hair short. Really short. It wasn't an act of rebellion, but a declaration of freedom. As the tresses fell to the floor, she felt the weight of years of "becoming" drop away. She was shedding the dead wood, pruning herself back so that the energy of her spirit could retreat to her core.

She hiked the local trails alone, her boots rhythmic against the packed earth, breathing in the scent of pine needles and ancient silence. Sometimes she talked out loud to herself, her voice a soft murmur against the canopy of trees. Sometimes she cried with no audience but the squirrels and the wind, letting the salt water of her grief irrigate the parched places of her heart. Other times, she just stood perfectly still on a ridge, eyes closed, letting the mountain breeze answer the questions she didn't yet know how to ask. She was learning that God often speaks loudest in the spaces where we stop talking.

She started writing again. Not to prove a point, not to publish a defiant blog post, and certainly not to counter the headlines that still flickered in the back of her mind. She wrote thoughts, prayers, introspective journal entries, and raw poetry. Some days the words flowed like a river after a thaw. Other days, the ink felt heavy, and all she could manage to scratch onto the paper was a single, defiant line: *"I am still here. I am still becoming."*

Her body began to find its own natural rhythm, independent of the stress that had governed it for so long. She put on a little weight, then lost some. She slept better, the kind of deep, restorative sleep that only comes when the conscience is clear. She drank water as if it were a holy rite, hydrating the cells that had been scorched by the fire of betrayal. She journaled until the pages ran out and the ink stained her fingertips.

And slowly, in the quiet of that Virginia cottage, she noticed the shift.

The ache that used to live in her chest, a constant, sharp pressure against her ribs, had grown quiet—a dull hum that eventually faded into the background.

The guilt that used to haunt her about the past—the "what ifs" and the "should haves" regarding Emily and the school—no longer knocked so loudly at the door of her mind. She realized she had been a good steward of the season, even if the season ended in a storm.

The craving to be seen, validated, or understood by the world? It had softened into a profound, unshakable peace. She no longer needed a golden crown to feel like royalty. She understood now that the most valuable crown is the one forged in the fire of resilience and worn in the sanctuary of the soul.

CHAPTER 22

THE PHONE CALL

The afternoon sun was beginning to dip, casting long, golden fingers across the porch of the cottage. I was sweeping, the rhythmic rasp of the bristles against the weathered wood acting as a form of meditation. Each stroke was an intentional clearing of the old dust, making room for the fresh mountain air to settle. My phone vibrated in my sweatshirt pocket—a sharp, sudden heartbeat against my hip. I pulled it out to find a number I didn't recognize, an unfamiliar area code that felt like a whisper from a world I had left behind.

"Hello?" I answered, my voice cautious, tethered to the stillness of the trees.

"Ma."

The single syllable hit me like a rain shower after a long drought. The voice on the other end was deeper than I remembered—richer, full of a resonance that spoke of miles traveled and obstacles overcome.

My son.

Deon.

He was calling from Europe. He had finally signed with a pro league team, a harvest he had sown in tears and hard work while I was fighting my own battles in the trenches. His voice sounded rested and confident, almost... healed. It was the sound of a tree that had survived a brutal winter and was finally putting forth its first green leaves of spring.

"I've been trying to find you," he said, and I could hear the faint echo of international lines between us. "You disappeared on me, Ma."

"I needed to disappear for a little while, baby," I replied, leaning against the porch railing, my eyes following the flight of a hawk circling above the foothills. "Not from you. Never from you. But from everything else. I needed to let my soil rest."

There was a long pause, a heavy silence filled with the years of sacrifice we had shared.

"I get it," he said softly. "I just needed you to know… I'm good. I'm actually happy, Ma. The game feels right again."

I closed my eyes, a single tear escaping to trace a path through the dust on my cheek. That one sentence filled me with more profound relief than any prestigious award or lottery check ever could. Hearing that his spirit was intact was the only crown I ever truly desired to wear.

"And Ma," he added, his voice thickening with a rare vulnerability, "you didn't fail. Not with the school. Not with the people who left. You gave people something to believe in when they had nothing left—including me. You planted seeds in us that are still growing, even if you aren't there to see the bloom."

My eyes welled up, the salt of my tears tasting like a holy cleansing.

We talked for an hour as the shadows grew long and the fireflies began to blink in the tall grass. We spoke about the complexity of life, about the weight of legacy, and about how dreams often look different than the blueprints we originally drew, yet they still count as a magnificent success. We talked about how the roots of our family had held firm even when the branches were being lashed by the storm.

Before we hung up, he said one last thing that anchored my soul to the earth:

"You taught me how to keep going even when people leave, even when the ones you trust most uproot themselves. You never said it out loud—you just lived it. I saw you keep your head up, Ma. I saw your crown."

I sat on the porch long after the line went silent, the phone still warm in my hand. The moon began to rise, silvering the edges of the hydrangeas Lila had planted.

I didn't need anything else that day. No explanations from the past, no apologies from those who had wronged me.

My son was whole.

And in the quiet of the Virginia night, I realized that I was, too.

CHAPTER 23

THE VISIT

It was unexpected, a sudden ripple in the quiet pool of my evening.

The knock at the door came just after sunset, when the sky was still bleeding with streaks of plum and fire—the remnants of a day that had burned itself out beautifully. I had been tucked into the corner of the couch, Lila's hand-stitched quilt draped across my legs, its weight a comforting reminder of the roots I had finally planted in my own soul. The sharp sound of knuckles against wood startled me, vibrating through the small room like an echo from a past I thought I had laid to rest.

I opened the door slowly, the cool mountain air rushing in to meet me.

Emily stood on the porch.

Her hair was longer now, falling in loose waves that seemed to lack their old, defiant luster. Her eyes looked tired, shadowed by a weariness that no amount of success could quite mask. A hesitant, fragile smile played at the corners of her mouth—a seedling trying to grow in rocky soil. I didn't speak at first. I just stood there, staring. The air between us buzzed with the static of all the things that hadn't been said, the years of silence that had grown like a thicket of thorns between two women who once shared everything.

"I was passing through," Emily said, her voice smaller than I remembered. "I... I thought about calling first. But I figured I owed you more than a digital ghost of a conversation. I owed it to the dirt we both came from to stand here in person."

I stepped aside, my heart steady but guarded. "You can come in, Emily."

We sat in the living room, the atmosphere cautious and heavy, like a house during a storm. The room was warm from the fireplace, but a chill still lingered in the space between our chairs. Emily finally spoke, her gaze drifting to the quilt on my lap, her fingers twisting a loose thread on her coat.

"I read about your new school. I saw the article in that small community paper... *Crown & Root*. That's a beautiful name, Crystal. It sounds like you. It sounds like someone who finally understands what holds a tree up."

"Thank you," I said, my voice a calm anchor. "It took a lot of pruning to get there."

Another pause stretched between us, long and agonizing.

"I came to say... I'm sorry," Emily said softly, her eyes finally meeting mine. They were swimming with a raw, unprotected honesty. "I know it doesn't change the harvest. I know it doesn't undo the fire. But I never wanted it to end the way it did. I was chasing a sun I thought I deserved, and I didn't care whose garden I trampled to get to it."

I looked at her for a long time, seeing the girl she used to be and the woman she had become. I saw the "Crown" she had tried to steal, and I realized it had never quite fit her head the way she hoped it would.

"I needed closure," Emily added, her voice cracking. "Not just for what I did to you... but for who I was when I did it. I couldn't breathe in my own house anymore."

I nodded slowly, a profound peace washing over me. It was the peace of a woman who no longer needed an apology to feel whole, but who could accept one as a gift of grace.

"I forgave you a long time ago, Emily," I said, and I meant it. I had released the debt in the secret places of my prayer closet months ago.

Emily exhaled, a ragged sound of relief that seemed to deflate her shoulders.

"But," I added gently, the "Calm Mentor" in me speaking with a firm, loving boundary, "that doesn't mean the season can be repeated. I've built something new now, Emily. I've tilled new soil, and I've learned to protect the perimeter of my peace. I've learned that not every branch that falls is meant to be grafted back on."

Emily nodded slowly, the truth of it settling between us like falling leaves. "I understand. I didn't come to ask for a seat at your table. I just came to tell you that you were right all along. The roots matter more than the gold."

We didn't cry. We didn't hug. We didn't try to force a bloom where the season had already passed. We didn't need to.

Sometimes, forgiveness is a boundary, not a bridge. It is the act of wishing someone well as they walk a different path, without feeling the need to follow them.

Emily left shortly after. There was no lingering drama, no grand promises of a future together. There was just a quiet, holy understanding that some stories end in silence, and that is its own kind of mercy. I watched her walk to her car, her silhouette disappearing into the Virginia night.

I closed the door and turned the lock, leaning my back against the wood. I realized then that not all doors should be reopened—even if the person on the other side has been forgiven. I walked back to the couch, pulled the quilt over my legs, and felt the deep, silent strength of my own roots holding me steady.

I was whole. I was standing. And for the first time, the crown didn't feel heavy at all.

CHAPTER 24

The Final Investment

Crystal sat at her kitchen table, the morning light filtered through the lace curtains of the cottage, casting patterns on the wood like the dappled shade of an old oak. Before her lay the remnants of a life measured in decimals and margins: a checkbook with a frayed cover, a savings ledger, and a spreadsheet she'd once used to manage a payroll that no longer existed. It all felt like echoes from a life that wasn't hers anymore—the dry husks of a season that had long since passed.

She could live simply now; the cottage life provided a quiet sanctuary, her part-time teaching offered a steady rhythm, and occasional consulting kept her mind sharp. But something stirred in the deep soil of her heart, a persistent tug that felt like a seed demanding to be planted. It was a need to do one last thing. Not to rebuild her own empire, but to help someone else find their light. A student named Bree had caught her attention, a young woman who reminded Crystal of a sapling that had survived a scorched forest.

Bree had lost both parents in a devastating house fire at seventeen. She worked two exhausting jobs, yet she still showed up to class with her notes highlighted in neon bursts of hope and her questions underlined with a hunger for a better life. Her dream was a beautiful, selfless thing: to open a mobile dental hygiene van to serve the rural, under-served areas where the lack of care left people in pain. She had the heart and the hands, but she didn't have the startup funds—the water needed to make the dream bloom.

Crystal opened her laptop, the screen glowing like a small hearth in the quiet room, and pulled up a small business grant application she had bookmarked months ago. Then, with a hand that didn't tremble, she reached for her checkbook and wrote a check from her personal account for $5,000.

It was a significant portion of what she had left, but it felt lighter than the money had ever felt when it was sitting in a bank. No strings were attached. No conditions were etched in the memo line.

Just belief.

Later that night, as the crickets began their rhythmic prayer in the tall grass outside, she slipped the check into an envelope along with a short, handwritten note:

"Bree, you don't owe me anything. Just promise to pass the light on one day when you see someone else standing in the dark. When someone believes in your roots before they see your crown, you build something far bigger than success—you build a legacy that the wind cannot blow away."

Crystal walked to the mailbox at the end of the gravel drive, the cool night air filling her lungs. The final investment of this season wasn't in a business plan or a corporate structure.

It was an investment in the faith that what you give away is the only thing you truly get to keep.

CHAPTER 25

THE SCRIPTURE ON THE WALL

Crystal stood in the front lobby of Crown & Root with a level, a pencil tucked behind her ear, and a framed piece of parchment clutched in her hands. The entryway had been freshly painted just days before—deep olive walls like the resilient leaves of a dormant oak, accented by brass sconces that threw warm, honeyed light across the space. A long bench sat against the wall, its cushions hand-stitched by local volunteers with fabrics that felt like home. It felt like a sacred space now. A threshold. A sanctuary where the heavy soil of the world could be shaken off, and burdens could be left at the door.

The parchment in her hand was aged, tea-stained by her own hand to give it a timeless, weathered feel. She had hand-lettered the scripture herself, choosing each brushstroke with a prayerful intention, the ink flowing like a steady stream. The words weren't just decorative—they were a declaration of her new foundation:

"For what shall it profit a man, if he shall gain the whole world, and lose his own soul?" — *Mark 8:36*

She measured the spot carefully, marking the wall with a light graphite stroke, and drilled the holes herself. The vibration of the tool in her hand felt like a clearing, a physical breaking through of the old to make way for the new. When she stepped back to admire the frame centered perfectly between the sconces, the weight of the scripture settled in her chest like an anchor—steadying, powerful, and deep.

The school was more than a classroom. It was more than job training or licensing preparation. It was a reclamation ground, a nursery for spirits that had been trampled by the storms of life. And that verse? It was the compass that would guide them through the thicket.

Later that afternoon, the sun dipped low, casting long shadows across the floorboards. Crystal stood behind the front desk, sipping ginger tea and reviewing enrollment packets, when she noticed a new student lingering by the framed scripture. Elijah.

He was twenty-three, quiet and thoughtful, with eyes that often looked like a troubled lake. He had a habit of taking notes even during casual conversation, as if he were afraid the truth might slip away if he didn't pin it to the page. He was the kind of student who sat in the back at first, arms crossed like a shield, but lately, he had begun leaning forward, his spirit reaching for the light as trust grew.

He was staring at the verse like it held a missing piece of his own story.

Crystal approached slowly, her footsteps soft on the floor, careful not to disrupt the quiet work the Holy Spirit was doing in his heart.

"It's a reminder," she said gently, her voice a calm melody in the still room.

Elijah turned toward her, his eyes glassy and bright. "I know this verse. My grandmother used to say it when I was younger, back when I was out there chasing the wrong things. She'd always tell me, 'Elijah, don't lose your soul chasing something that won't hug you back.'"

Crystal smiled, feeling the warmth of that inherited wisdom. "She sounds like she knew exactly where her roots were planted."

"She was a rock," he said, his voice thick with a sudden, raw emotion. "But I didn't listen. I thought I needed the world. I didn't realize how much of myself I was giving away until I lost everything."

He didn't elaborate on the fire he had walked through, and she didn't press. She knew that some roots need time in the dark before they are ready to be uncovered.

"You're here now," she said, resting a hand briefly on his shoulder. "That means you're choosing a different harvest. You're choosing the gold that doesn't tarnish."

Elijah nodded, exhaling a long, shaky breath. "I needed this today. I needed to remember why I'm starting over."

As the seasons of the school year began to turn, Crystal noticed more and more students stopping by the framed scripture. Some took photos with their phones, wanting to carry the light home. Others ran their fingers across the glass, tracing the letters as if they were Braille for the soul. A few even asked if she had more verses posted around the building, hungry for more than just technical knowledge.

Crystal began leaving small index cards in a hand-carved wooden dish beneath the frame—tiny seeds of light. Each one was handwritten with a different passage of encouragement.

They disappeared by the dozen.

One student, Teresa, began taping them inside her locker door, making her own small altar. Another, Brian, started using them as bookmarks in his technical workbooks, letting the Word keep his place. The scripture had become a silent teacher—one that didn't test or lecture, but offered a cool drink of water when the world got loud and parched.

Weeks later, a guest speaker visited for a student development workshop. He was a recruiter from a prestigious dental firm, a man of sharp suits and quick words, but also a former pastor who still carried the scent of the pulpit. When he stepped into the entryway and saw the framed verse, he paused mid-stride, his professional mask slipping for a moment.

"You don't see this in schools anymore," he said, turning to Crystal. "It's bold. In today's world, it's almost a risk."

"It's not a risk; it's a necessity," Crystal replied, her voice steady and unbowed. "We aren't just teaching them how to fix teeth. We're teaching them how to stand tall."

He nodded, his voice dropping to a reverent, conversational tone. "It sets the tone. It tells them that the root of the matter is the heart. You've built something different here, Crystal."

That night, after the last student had departed and the building was wrapped in the velvet silence of evening, Crystal stood alone before the frame. The lobby was quiet, lit only by the soft, amber glow of the sconces. She reached out and touched the glass, her fingers resting over the word *soul*.

She remembered what it felt like to lose her own soul piece by piece, back when the first school felt like an empire and betrayal made her question her very worth. She remembered when ambition had tempted her to overwork and overgive until she was a hollow shell of the woman God made her to be. Back then, she had the "whole world" on paper—the awards, the recognition, the growth—but she felt bankrupt in private.

Now, she had less in the eyes of the world, but her spirit was overflowing. The "Mama Crown" she once wore for others had been replaced by a crown of peace that sat light on her head because it was rooted in the Truth.

She turned off the lights, the darkness feeling like a warm embrace, and whispered, "Thank You. For bringing me back to the garden. For bringing me back to what matters."

And in the hush of that holy moment, the scripture didn't just hang on the wall—it echoed in every fiber of her being.

A soul restored.□

A legacy realigned.□

And a school rooted in a soil that no headline or betrayal could ever take away.

CHAPTER 26

THE LETTER FROM THE PAST

It arrived in a plain white envelope, unassuming and humble, like a seed waiting for the right season to break the surface.

There was no return address. No stamps with anything fancy—just a standard mark from a post office a few towns over. My name was typed in a stark block font, but there was a slight smudge on the bottom corner, a faint fingerprint of oil or ink that suggested it had been handled with nervous, trembling fingers.

I turned it over in my hands before opening it, the paper feeling cool against my skin. The air in the room seemed to shift, growing still and expectant. It was that quiet recognition deep in my gut—a whisper from the Spirit—that this wasn't junk mail or a bill. This was a message from a season I thought had long since turned to autumn.

Inside were three things: a typed letter, a folded brochure from the BrightSmile Institute, and a Polaroid photograph of a young woman standing at a podium in a vibrant lavender graduation gown. My breath hitched as I began to read:

"Dear Ms. Crystal,

You may not remember me. I was one of the many who left Crown Point during the chaos. To be honest, I was scared. I was confused. Everything felt like a forest fire, and I didn't know which way to run to save my future. I believed what others said without asking questions because their voices were louder. I transferred to BrightSmile. I graduated there. But my roots... my roots started with you."

I read the words slowly, the syllables catching in my throat like dry leaves.

"You saw me when I didn't know I could be seen. You looked at my quietness and told me my silence was still powerful—that a tree doesn't have to roar to be strong. You told me not to be afraid of entering rooms that didn't look like me, to carry my own light into the dark. I didn't understand the weight of that then. But I do now."

The letter went on to describe how she had become licensed, the pride she felt in her pediatric dental clinic, and how she kept a tattered picture of Crown Point's first-day flyer taped inside her locker—the one I had handed out door-to-door in the driving rain, my own spirit damp but determined.

"I didn't know the full story back then," the letter ended, the ink slightly blurred on the final line. *"But I know now. I know who poured the first water into my soil. I know who made me believe I was more than the dirt I came from. Thank you. You didn't just teach us a trade, Ms. Crystal. You planted a legacy."*

I set the letter down on my desk, my hands shaking. I picked up the Polaroid. The young woman in the photo had tears shimmering in her eyes. She was captured mid-speech, her mouth open in a beautiful expression of joy or conviction—perhaps both. She looked like a woman who finally knew the strength of her own crown.

And for the first time in weeks, I wept.

It wasn't the weeping of grief or the jagged sobbing of betrayal. These were the tears of a gardener seeing the first bloom of a tree she thought had been lost to the frost.

The investment had returned.

It hadn't come back in dollars or dividends. It had returned in destiny. It was proof that even when the storms of life tear the branches away, the seeds we plant in others with love and integrity are protected beneath the soil.

I folded the letter carefully, smoothing the creases with my thumb. I walked over to my small keepsake box—the one that held the charred remains of my old business plan and Deon's NBA draft hat. I placed the letter inside, a fresh layer of hope for my own foundation, and whispered to the quiet room:

"Legacy doesn't need to be loud to be lasting. It just needs to live."

And in that holy moment, as the sun dipped below the Virginia hills, I felt it living within me.

CHAPTER 27
THE LOCAL AWARD

The email arrived on a rainy Thursday morning, the kind of day where the sky is a soft, bruised purple and the world feels as though it's being quietly washed clean. Crystal was sipping peppermint tea by the front window of her cottage, the steam rising in gentle, translucent curls that mimicked the mist clinging to the hydrangea bushes outside. She watched the droplets race down the glass, thinking of how the earth needs the rain to soften the soil before the next season's bloom. When the notification chimed softly on her phone, she almost ignored it—most messages these days were digital noise, newsletters or spam that felt like weeds in her mental garden.

But the subject line caught her eye:

Subject: Congratulations, Ms. Jameson—You've Been Selected

She opened it with a cautious, held breath. Inside was an invitation to the annual *Women in Impact* banquet hosted by the local Chamber of Progress, a modest but longstanding event recognizing the quiet heroes who labored in the fields of education, health, and community service.

"You've been nominated and selected as a recipient of this year's Resilience and Renewal Award," the letter read. "We would be honored to celebrate your contributions to our region through the Crown & Root Institute."

Crystal blinked at the screen, a sudden warmth spreading through her chest that had nothing to do with the tea. She had never pursued accolades. In fact, after the collapse of Crown Point Academy—the fire that had nearly consumed her spirit—she had shied away from anything that smelled of ceremony or the blinding glare of a spotlight. She had preferred the shade. But this... this felt like the earth finally acknowledging the roots she had painstakingly replanted in the dark.

She reread the letter twice more, her eyes lingering on the word *Renewal*. She forwarded it to Lorraine with a short note: *Do you know anything about this?*

Lorraine's reply came back almost instantly, accompanied by a winking emoji and a single, defiant sentence: *Told them everything. About time the world saw the fruit, not just the fence.*

The night of the banquet arrived with the swiftness of a changing season.

Crystal stood in front of the full-length mirror, her fingers trembling slightly as she adjusted the sleeves of a dress she hadn't worn in years. It was navy silk, a deep, cool shade like the midnight sky, simple but elegant. It was borrowed from Lorraine, who had arrived early and insisted on doing Crystal's makeup, her hands steady and sure. As Crystal looked at her reflection, she saw the silver earrings catching the light like distant stars. For the first time in a long time, she looked at the woman in the glass without the sharp edge of critique.

"I look... calm," she whispered to the quiet room. She didn't look like a woman wearing a heavy, golden crown for show; she looked like a woman whose dignity was woven into her very skin.

She arrived at the banquet hall just before the sun dipped below the horizon. The venue wasn't grand—it was a repurposed old courthouse with high ceilings and string lights that draped overhead like a canopy of fireflies. The folding chairs were covered in white satin, but the space glowed with a raw, shared intention. Women from all over the county filled the room; some were in sharply tailored power suits, others in cherished, thrifted dresses, all gathered to honor stories that had rarely been told outside of kitchen tables and prayer closets.

Crystal sat at a table near the stage, sipping cool water and scanning the program. She recognized no one by name, and yet, looking at the tired but triumphant eyes around her, she felt completely at home. They were all gardeners of their own lives.

When her name was finally called, the applause wasn't the deafening roar of a stadium. It was warm. It was earnest. It was the sound of a community recognizing a testimony.

She stepped up to the small stage, her heels clicking softly against the old wood floor, a sound that reminded her of the rhythm of a steady heart. A bouquet of wildflowers was placed in her arms—messy, vibrant, and real. The microphone was adjusted. The spotlight gently found her, not as a harsh interrogator, but as a soft light illuminating a survivor.

She hadn't prepared a speech. She hadn't even allowed herself to think of what she might say. But as she looked out at the faces, her voice didn't waver. It was the voice of a mentor who had survived the storm.

"I didn't come here to be known," she said slowly, her words carrying the weight of her journey. "I came here to do something that mattered. To show women that they are still worthy of becoming, even after the betrayal has tried to uproot them. Even after the breakdown has left them feeling like scorched earth. Tonight, I don't just feel seen... I feel r ooted."

She paused, swallowing the knot of emotion that felt like a holy thing in her throat.

"Thank you for honoring the roots, not just the crown."

The room stood. They clapped not just for her, but for the universal truth of the journey they sensed in her. Afterward, people approached her one by one, like travelers seeking a drink from a well. A social worker shared how Crystal's school had helped a client find her footing again. A librarian mentioned she'd heard the students at Crown & Root talking about their futures with a new kind of pride.

Then, a young girl—barely eighteen, with eyes that reminded Crystal of herself years ago—stepped forward and whispered, "I want to start something one day, too. I didn't think I could after what happened to me. But you did."

Crystal smiled, holding the girl's hand for a moment. "The soil is always ready for a new seed, honey. You just have to trust the growth."

When the night ended and the last of the lights dimmed, Crystal returned to her car. The award plaque rested in her lap, its weight comforting. It wasn't gold. It wasn't covered in glitter or faux gems. It was made of wood—dark, polished oak, grounded and simple. Just like her.

At home, she didn't place it on a pedestal in the center of the room. Instead, she hung it on the wall of her office, tucked beside Denisha's letter and the very first, rain-smudged flyer from Crown Point Academy.

She stared at the collection—the pain, the promise, and the proof.

"Let them say whatever they want," she whispered to the stillness of the cottage. "This—this is the truth that speaks loudest. The roots held. The crown is light."

CHAPTER 28

THE DREAM REVISITED

That night, the dream returned—unexpected, soft around the edges, like a memory dipped in honey and held up to the golden hour light. Crystal had gone to sleep with the windows of her Virginia cottage propped open, allowing a gentle summer breeze to curl its way through the white linen curtains. It was a night for deep resting, for allowing the soil of the soul to lie fallow. She had drifted off while reading a book she never quite finished, a story of restoration she'd been sipping on for weeks. But what came to her in the velvet dark was not the plot of any earthly book.

It was a vision of a place her heart once called home—Crown Point Academy.

But in this dream, the building wasn't shuttered, dim, or draped in the gray dust of litigation. It was vibrantly, breathlessly alive.

The halls were polished and bright, reflecting the morning sun like a calm lake. The walls were freshly painted in warm neutrals and deep, regal blues—colors that felt like an embrace. The familiar, clean scent of lavender and lemon cleaner hung in the air, and the floors shone with a kind of quiet reverence. Crystal walked through the building slowly, her steps silent, as if she were floating just an inch off the ground, a spirit returning to a garden it had once tended.

Laughter, bright and unfiltered, rang from the classrooms. Through the glass of the doors, she saw students sitting at desks, leaning in, their faces illuminated with engagement and a notebook-full of purpose. The lights flickered not with the stutter of age, but with a warm, steady hum. As she passed Room 3, she paused. She heard the soft voice of a student whispering to another, "That's Ms. Crystal's quote on the wall—she used to say it every Monday like a prayer."

"You are not here to survive. You are here to rise."

Crystal felt a surge of heat in her chest, a restorative fire that didn't burn but healed. She stepped into the front office, the heart of the school. And there she saw her. Emily.

She wasn't the woman Crystal last saw—hardened, distant, eyes shielded by the weight of a stolen crown. In the dream, she was softer. Her eyes were kinder, reflecting the clarity of a sky after a long, purging storm. Her shoulders were no longer tense with the burden of duplicity. Emily stood behind the front desk, reorganizing folders and humming a soft, familiar melody to herself.

Crystal didn't speak. Neither did Emily.

They simply looked at one another, two women who had once shared a single canopy before the lightning strike. There was no animosity, no lingering smoke from the fire, no sorrow for the branches that had been torn away. There was only a knowing—a quiet, subterranean truce, the kind of peace that only time and the grace of God could forge.

Emily smiled faintly, a small, humble nod of acknowledgment. And Crystal, feeling the last of the frost melt from her heart, returned it.

She turned and walked back down the hall, toward the double doors that led to the world outside. As she stepped across the threshold, she was met with a sun that was not blinding or harsh, but golden and forgiving.

She paused on the steps, took one long look back at the brick and mortar, and saw the new sign hanging proudly above the door: *Crown Point Academy — Where Roots and Crowns Begin.*

She smiled, a deep, soul-level curve of the lips.

Then, she woke up.

The morning light stretched across her bedroom in long, shimmering ribbons—a gentle invitation to the day. She blinked into consciousness, her hand still resting peacefully on her pillow, her breath as calm as the mountain air outside.

She didn't cry. She didn't feel the old, familiar pull of grief or the sharp jab of "what might have been."

She whispered aloud, her voice clear and certain in the morning hush, "I'm free."

And for the first time in years, she meant it in the marrow of her bones. Not because she had forgotten the pain, and not because the past had miraculously rewritten its own jagged edges. She was free because she was no longer carrying the heavy weight of the building, the betrayal, or the "Mama Crown" mantle she had worn for everyone but herself.

The dream wasn't just nostalgia. It was a holy permission.

It was permission to believe that even broken beginnings can carry beautiful endings, and that a garden can still be beautiful even after the gardener has moved on. In that moment, she knew the truth she would carry to her students at Crown & Root:

Peace doesn't always arrive with the herald of trumpets or the roar of a storm. Sometimes, it tiptoes in with a smile in the middle of a dream and leaves you lighter than you were before the sun rose.

CHAPTER 29

A LEGACY ON PAPER

The cursor blinked on the screen like a patient heartbeat, steady and expectant. Crystal stared at the empty white field of the state board newsletter submission portal, the subject line pre-filled in a sterile font: *Why I Teach*. She had almost ignored the email altogether, letting it sit in her inbox like a fallen leaf on a porch. There had been too many urgent to-do lists lately—the daily pruning of semester evaluations, a building inspection that felt like checking the strength of her own walls, and two grant reports that required the clinical language of numbers rather than the language of the soul.

Writing a blurb for a statewide publication didn't exactly scream urgent in the face of a leaking faucet or a student's failing grade. But something in the quiet, honey-lit moments of her morning, as the steam rose from her tea and the world outside the Virginia cottage remained hushed, pushed her back to the keyboard.

She looked out the window of her office into the common area of the school. A student named Kierra was hunched over a workstation, patiently walking a younger classmate through the delicate architecture of a dental mold. Their voices were soft, a low murmur of mentorship filled with occasional ripples of laughter. Lorraine buzzed through the hallway, the brisk snap of her footsteps echoing with purpose as she handed out newly laminated ID cards with the pride of someone distributing a royal decree.

The rhythm of the school moved now without Crystal needing to micromanage every beat. It was breathing on its own. It was living. It was a forest that had found its own ecosystem, and she had been the one to clear the brush and till the earth to make it possible.

Her fingers, calloused by years of labor and softened by the grace of her journey, began to move across the keys.

"I teach because someone once showed me that the dirt I came from didn't determine the height of my bloom."

She paused. Reread the line. It felt honest, a raw truth pulled from the deep soil of her memory.

Then the recollections rushed in, a flood of faces and voices from the years before the fire. She thought of her old high school science teacher, Mr. Walton, a man who saw past her quiet exterior and the poverty of her circumstances. He had handed her a dog-eared, spine-cracked book on anatomy with a look of solemn belief, saying, "This is for you, Crystal. I think you're meant to build something that matters. Don't let the world tell you otherwise." She had carried that book in her backpack for a year, the edges of the pages curling like dried petals, but the words inside acting as a map for her spirit.

She thought of the very first student who had ever looked her in the eyes and called her "Mama C." The nickname had stuck like a burr, persistent and familiar. She had never asked for the title, but she realized now it was love disguised as familiarity—a respect that didn't require a plaque or a podium. Crystal kept typing, the words flowing like a river after a heavy rain:

"I teach because too many women are conditioned to believe that their value is merely decorative—a flower meant for a vase, rather than a tree meant for the sky. They are told their intelligence is an accessory and that their voice is either too much or not nearly enough. I teach because I believe in building sacred spaces where those lies are unraveled, where the crown is reclaimed, and where the roots are finally allowed to go deep."

The words were no longer hesitant; she was in the current now, the "Calm Mentor" speaking through her fingertips.

"I teach because I know the freezing cold of being overlooked. I know the jagged edge of being betrayed by those you once called sisters. I know what it's like to have your vision dismissed until someone else wears your hard work like their own stolen crown. But even after the storm has leveled the field, I still believe in the holy work of sowing. I believe in showing up, even when the heart is weary. I believe in shaping futures that aren't built on the shifting sands of power, but on the bedrock of purpose."

She looked at the word count. It was double what the editors had requested.

She didn't care. Some truths couldn't be trimmed for the sake of a margin.

At the end of the piece, she added one final line, a quiet exhale of her own resilient spirit:

"I continue because somewhere, right now, someone else is standing in the dark, and they still need to believe that they can rise too."

She clicked **SUBMIT**.

Then, instead of logging off to tackle the next fire on her desk, she did something impulsive. She printed a copy. She watched the machine spit out the warm paper, the ink still fresh. She walked it down the hallway, the scent of the school—a mix of sterile equipment and the sweet perfume of hope—surrounding her. She took a piece of tape and pressed the essay onto the staff lounge bulletin board, right in the center.

She didn't do it for credit. She didn't do it so they would praise her.

She did it for courage—their courage and her own.

Every person in that building was a branch of her legacy. It wasn't written in ink or carved into awards, but etched into the quiet belief they now held in themselves. And Crystal knew, as she walked back to her office with her head held high, that belief was exactly how the crown stayed rooted.

CHAPTER 30

TEA WITH MISS LILA

The porch at Miss Lila's cottage had always felt like a sanctuary—quiet, strong, and a weathered witness to decades of joy and sorrow. It was a place where people didn't rush, where the frantic ticking of the world's clock seemed to slow down and listen to the wind. Today, the wicker chair groaned softly beneath me, a familiar, comforting sound as I sat wrapped in a thick wool shawl. I watched the steam from my teacup curl like a silken ribbon into the crisp afternoon air, feeling the cool Virginia breeze kiss my cheeks.

Miss Lila emerged from the kitchen, a tray balanced effortlessly on her hand. It held two mismatched porcelain teacups—one painted with delicate violets, the other with a fading gold rim—a heavy ceramic pot of herbal tea, and a small plate of lemon cookies dusted with sugar. Her steps across the porch boards were slow but certain, a gentle, percussive rhythm that comforted me more than I had the words to explain.

"You picked the cinnamon blend," Miss Lila said as she poured the amber liquid. The scent was warm and earthy, like the very roots of the mountains. "You always do when the soil of your spirit is stirred up."

I smiled softly, feeling the heat of the cup transfer to my palms. "Is it that obvious, Lila?"

"It is," she replied, taking the seat beside me and settling in with a sigh of contentment. "Your silence says more than most people's words, Crystal. It's a deep water, but I can see the ripples."

We sat in companionable quiet for a few minutes, sipping our tea. In the distance, a blue jay called out from the pines, and the occasional creak of the wooden floorboards beneath our shifting weight filled the stillness. I looked out toward the horizon, where the mountains sat like sleeping giants draped in velvet green.

"I saw the article," Miss Lila said gently, her voice barely louder than the rustle of the leaves. "The one about your school. That picture of you standing in front of Crown & Root with those students gathered around you... you looked like a woman who had finally found her true North."

I nodded, my fingers tightening slightly around the porcelain. "It still feels unreal sometimes. Like I'm living in a garden I once dreamed of but didn't think I deserved to walk in anymore. After the fire at Crown Point, I thought the ground was too scorched for anything else to grow."

Miss Lila reached over and placed her hand on mine—her skin felt like soft, sun-warmed parchment. "You didn't just survive the fire, Crystal. You learned that some seeds only crack open when the heat gets high enough. You didn't just rebuild; you learned how to burn with a light that doesn't consume you. Not many can say they've been refined like that."

My eyes brimmed with sudden, hot tears. "I was so close to giving up, Lila. I was ready to let the hurt become my identity, to let the betrayal be the only story I told. But every time I watched one of my students stand a little taller, I found another reason to stay grounded. I realized that if I let my roots wither, they wouldn't have anything to hold onto."

"That's because you were never just teaching them dental tech, baby," Miss Lila said, her eyes twinkling with a sharp, ancient wisdom. "You were reminding yourself of your own worth. You were proving to your own soul that your crown wasn't lost in the ashes. It was just being reshaped into something more durable. Something made of heartwood instead of just gold."

We drank in silence for a while, the weight of those words settling over us like late-afternoon sunlight. I looked out over the yard where spring had begun its slow, miraculous bloom. The dogwood trees stood tall, their white blossoms like stars, their branches reaching like arms to the sky.

"I wonder if it will always feel like this," I murmured, my voice a soft confession. "This strange mix of grief and gratitude. Like I'm still mourning the branches that were stripped away at Crown Point, even while I'm celebrating the fruit that's growing here."

Miss Lila gave a soft, knowing chuckle. "That's exactly what a life of faith is, Crystal. It's a quilt of contradictions—remember the one I gave you? Pain is stitched right beside peace, and the thread of grace is what holds it all together. It's the tension that keeps us warm."

I exhaled, feeling my shoulders drop an inch lower, releasing a tension I hadn't realized I was still holding.

"You're not done becoming, Crystal," Miss Lila added after a moment, her gaze fixed on the setting sun. "But don't try to force the blossoms. Don't rush the next chapter. Let it rise like bread in the oven. Slow. Sure. And worth the wait."

We finished our tea as the sun began its slow, majestic descent behind the hills, painting the sky in strokes of violet and gold. As I stood to leave, Miss Lila pulled me into a hug. She smelled of lavender and old books, a scent that meant *home*.

"You're not just surviving anymore, Crystal Jameson," she whispered into my ear. "You're thriving. That's what a beautiful rebuilding looks like."

I walked away from the porch with a smile that felt different—a smile that carried more healing than a thousand apologies from the past ever could. I knew then that sometimes, the greatest peace doesn't come in the form of an answer or an apology, but in the simple, holy act of being seen—fully, gently, and without needing to explain the scars.

CHAPTER 31

DENISHA'S GRADUATION

The gymnasium at Crown & Root had never felt more alive—a vibrant greenhouse where the final harvest of the season was being gathered. It wasn't an expansive space, and there were no grand chandeliers or blinding stadium lights to herald the occasion. Instead, there were neat rows of simple folding chairs, a small stage draped in gold-and-purple streamers that shivered in the afternoon breeze, and a makeshift wooden podium Crystal had borrowed from the local community center. But the atmosphere? That was electric, charged with the holy current of people who had survived the fire and were finally ready to bloom.

Families packed the space until the air was thick with the scent of floral perfumes and hairspray. Babies bounced on hips, their gurgles a sweet counterpoint to the rustle of programs; cousins snapped photos with eager flashes, and friends waved across the aisles, their voices rising in a joyful hum. Crystal stood backstage, partially hidden by a velvet curtain, taking it all in. Her heart pounded with a familiar anticipation—not the frantic nerves of her younger years, but a deep, bone-deep pride. It was the feeling of a gardener seeing the first green shoots of a long-awaited spring.

This was the second graduating class of Crown & Root Institute.

It wasn't a massive group—only seventeen students—but each one carried a story that deserved a parade of its own. They were recovering addicts who had fought for clarity, formerly incarcerated men and women reclaiming their place in the sun, single parents who had studied by the light of the refrigerator while their children slept. They were survivors. They were dreamers. They were fighters who had refused to be uprooted by the storms. And then, there was Denisha.

She was the one Crystal watched most closely.

Quiet. Sharp. Consistent. Denisha was a young woman who moved through the world with a careful, guarded grace. She had never missed a class, rarely spoke unless she had weighed her words like gold, and always turned in her work early, the pages crisp and perfect. She wore her past pain like a well-pressed blazer—tidy, buttoned-up, and protective. But every once in a while, during a lecture on anatomy or a quiet moment in the lab, Crystal had seen the softness behind her eyes, the vulnerability of a budding flower hoping the frost was finally gone.

When her name was finally called, Denisha walked toward the stage, her steps slow but anchored with a new confidence. Her mortarboard was decorated with glittering letters that caught the light: *"Still Rising."* Her mother stood in the back row, weeping openly into a lace handkerchief, surrounded by family members who clapped with a fervor that suggested they were welcoming home a hero. Crystal handed her the certificate—that small, powerful parchment of peace—but instead of a formal handshake, Denisha pulled her into a hug. A long one. A healing one.

"You didn't just save my education," Denisha whispered into Crystal's ear, her voice trembling. "You saved me. You showed me my roots were enough."

Crystal blinked back her own tears, her hand resting on the small of the girl's back. "You were already strong, Denisha. I just reminded you to reach for the light. The crown stays secure when the roots are deep—that's how we stay crowned."

After the ceremony, the gymnasium transformed into a banquet of celebration. The air changed, now smelling of the lemon cake and savory potluck dishes brought in by proud families. Crystal sat at a small table near the back, content to be the quiet observer of the joy she had helped cultivate. Denisha eventually found her way over, her gown rustling as she sat down, the tassel on her cap swinging.

"Can I ask you something?" Denisha said, her fingers nervously fiddling with the edge of her diploma.

"Of course, honey."

"How did you know what to say to us? In class, I mean. You always knew when someone needed a word of encouragement, or just some space, or maybe a little bit of both."

Crystal smiled, the expression reaching her eyes. "Because I have been in the dry places, too, Denisha. I know what it feels like to have the world try to prune you back to nothing. I just became what I wish someone had been for me during my winter. I learned that we are all just planting in tears, hoping to reap in joy."

Denisha nodded, a look of profound understanding crossing her face. "You did that. For all of us."

They sat together for a while, sharing a plate of lemon cake and dreaming about what lay ahead. Denisha had plans to apply for a position at a pediatric dental clinic, but her eyes truly lit up when she spoke of her ultimate goal: opening a nonprofit for teen moms who wanted to study dental tech, creating a nursery for the dreams of others.

"You'll do it," Crystal said, her voice filled with a certainty that required no proof. "Just remember to lead with your heart, not just your hustle. Let your roots provide the power, and the crown will take care of itself."

That night, after the last car had pulled out of the parking lot and the gold-and-purple decorations had been carefully packed away for the next season, Crystal walked the length of the silent gymnasium alone.

She touched the worn wood of the podium, ran her fingers across the "Crown & Root" banner, and whispered a silent prayer into the rafters: *Let this work always matter more than the credit, Lord. Let these students outgrow us in the best way. Let them be oaks of righteousness.*

As she turned off the lights, she looked back one more time at the empty room. It no longer looked like a gym; it looked like a sanctuary that had held the weight of seventeen miracles. Denisha would go on to succeed in the world, certainly. But more importantly, she would go on to believe in her own worth.

And that belief was the ultimate harvest. That was what made every struggle, every betrayal, and every tear worth the cost.

CHAPTER 32

THE NEW HIRE

The office smelled of fresh paint and lemon oil, a clean, sharp scent that always felt like a new beginning to me—a clearing away of old dust to make room for fresh growth. Crown & Root had matured from a humble, quiet reawakening into a fully operational, spirit-driven institute, teeming with lives being carefully replanted. I stood by the front window, my fingers wrapped around the steady warmth of my herbal tea, watching through the glass as students filed through the main doors below. Their shadows stretched long across the pavement, each one a living story in progress. Most days were a quiet blur of class prep, the holy work of mentoring, and the necessary pruning of paperwork—but this day carried a specific, shimmering excitement. Today, I was interviewing for my first Assistant Director.

I hadn't rushed the process. After everything I had been through, I knew that you cannot graft just any branch onto a healthy tree; the spirit of the wood has to match. I'd posted the listing quietly, like a prayer whispered into the wind, reviewed the resumes by hand, and called each reference personally to listen for the things they *didn't* say. I wasn't looking for a perfect resume or a clinical list of achievements. I was looking for someone real. Someone who believed that education was a form of healing. Someone who understood that you have to tend to the roots if you ever want to see a crown. The final interview was with a young woman named Alicia Monroe.

Alicia was twenty-nine, a graduate of a sister tech institute out of Raleigh. Her resume was solid, but what had truly caught my spirit was the handwritten note she'd scrawled at the bottom of her cover letter:

"I'm not applying to be part of a brand—I'm applying to be part of a movement. I want to grow with someone who knows what it feels like to rebuild from the ground up."

That line had stayed with me, a resonant chord that hummed in the back of my mind for days.

When Alicia walked in for her interview, her energy was a steady, open light. She wore a navy blazer over a sunflower-yellow blouse—a bright bloom of hope that made me smile—and her natural hair was styled in a curly bob that framed her face with a quiet, grounded confidence. I stood to greet her, feeling a strange sense of recognition, as if we were two trees sharing the same soil.

"You look like you belong here already," I said, and the words felt like a blessing.

Alicia smiled, her eyes bright and honest. "I've been hoping you'd say that, Ms. Crystal."

We sat across from each other in my office, the sunlight spilling across the desk like liquid gold. Instead of diving straight into the sterile checkboxes of job requirements, I began with a simple prompt—the kind of question that bypasses the ego and goes straight to the spirit:

"Tell me who you are, Alicia—not just what you've done."

Alicia took a deep, centering breath and began to speak, her voice a soft but sturdy current.

"I'm someone who knows what it feels like to be underestimated. I know the sting of having people look at your past and assume they've already written your future. I was told I'd never finish my own schooling because I had to drop out for a year to be the hands and feet for my mother when she got sick. I was told I was 'too soft' to be a leader, as if kindness were a weakness instead of a root. I've been overlooked and I've been underpaid—but I never stopped believing I had a holy purpose. I want to be in a place that doesn't just see that purpose, but knows how to multiply it in others."

I listened with my whole heart. Every word she spoke echoed the silent prayers I had whispered in that diner booth years ago. I didn't need to see any more certificates or hear any more references.

"You're hired," I said, standing to shake her hand. I felt a surge of peace, a settling in my chest. "Let's build something that doesn't just stand, but lasts."

Alicia's eyes widened, her professional mask slipping into a look of pure, joyful shock. "Just like that?"

I smiled, the "Calm Mentor" in me feeling more certain than ever. "I have learned to trust my spirit more than I trust a standard procedure. And my spirit says you're part of this next chapter. You're exactly the kind of gardener this school needs."

Within a week, Alicia had fully stepped into the rhythm of the role. She brought a much-needed structure to our systems and a fresh, vibrant voice to our staff meetings. She carried a calm boldness that balanced my own seasoned intuition, acting as a sturdy trellis for my vision. We worked together like a beautiful melody—different notes, but perfectly aligned in the same key.

On the anniversary of her first month, I left a handwritten note on her desk, tucked beside a small succulent I'd chosen for her. *"You don't just support the vision, Alicia. You expand it. Thank you for showing up in your full, beautiful bloom."*

Alicia framed that note and placed it where she could see it every morning.

And for the first time in a very long time, I felt a weight lift from my shoulders. I realized that the crown I was carrying was no longer mine to bear alone. I had found a partner whose roots were as deep as my own.

Together, we weren't just running a school. We were cultivating a movement of restoration. A new chapter had truly begun—not just for the building of Crown & Root, but for the women who were building it, brick by brick and heart by heart.

CHAPTER 33

A Letter to Herself

On her forty-fourth birthday, Crystal didn't plan a party. There were no crowded brunches, no scheduled spa days, and no performative social media posts featuring shimmering balloon numbers. Instead, she spent the morning wrapped in the familiar embrace of her favorite plush robe, sipping warm tea on the porch of the home she and her husband had built—a structure of wood and light that stood as a testament to a restored life.

The sky above the Virginia hills was painted a soft, introspective gray. It was the kind of sky that holds memory, a vast canvas for a soul that has weathered the storm. That morning, the air felt heavy with the scent of damp earth and the promise of an April awakening. Crystal lit a lavender candle, its flame dancing with a quiet, steady resolve. She opened a fresh journal, the blank pages smelling of possibilities and new soil, and began to write a letter. It wasn't a message for a friend, her son, or even her husband. This was a letter to the woman she had once been and the woman she was still becoming.

She dated it carefully: *April 8th, Year 44.*

Then, slowly and deliberately, her pen began to glide across the paper, the ink flowing like a river after a spring thaw:

Dear Me,

You have carried too much for too long, yet here you are—still standing, still rooted. You have forgiven what didn't ask for forgiveness, proving that grace is not a transaction, but a transformation. You have pushed through the hard clay of betrayal to find the sun. You have loved again, even when love required your vulnerability, your fears, and the tender exposure of your scars.

You once thought the collapse of the old school was the end of the forest. But it wasn't. It was simply the fire that cleared the brush, making way for a different kind of building—slower, softer, and infinitely more sacred. It is the kind of building that doesn't hunger for validation, for it is fed by vision. You are not the lies they told. You are not the person who was left behind in the wreckage. You are not what they wrote in sensational headlines or the whispers that echoed in rooms where your name was used as a cautionary tale.

You are the choice you made next.

You didn't fight to prove you were right; you built to prove you were whole. You didn't wear your crown to prove your power; you tended your roots to prove your purpose.

You are not healed simply because the pain stopped. You are healed because you refused to let the hurt stop your blooming. I am proud of you.

You survived grief without letting it petrify your heart. You survived success without letting it intoxicate your spirit into arrogance. You survived the "in-between"—that terrifying wilderness where most people get stuck—and you turned it into a sanctuary. You are, finally, home. Not just in this house, but in yourself.

Love always,

Yourself

When she finished, Crystal folded the letter with a gentle precision. She placed it in a wooden box on the small side table, a container marked "Sacred Things." Inside were the fragments of her journey: a few old, curled photos; a program from the final, bittersweet graduation at Crown Point Academy; the very first flyer from Crown & Root, slightly wrinkled from the rain; and the necklace her son had given her, a small gold circle that felt like a completed cycle.

She sat back in the wicker chair, tears welling in her eyes—not from the jagged edge of sadness, but from a deep, honoring gratitude. It was the kind of peace that only comes when you finally stop running from your reflection and decide to love the woman looking back.

The door behind her creaked softly. Her husband appeared in the doorway, holding two steaming mugs of cocoa, his presence a warm anchor. He wore a smile that suggested he knew exactly how much work it had taken for her to reach this plateau of peace.

"Writing again?" he asked softly, handing her a mug.

"Just to myself," she said, her voice a steady melody in the morning air.

"Well," he said, leaning down to kiss her on the forehead, the scent of chocolate and home surrounding them, "I hope you told her how amazing she is. I hope you told her she's the strongest oak I've ever seen."

Crystal smiled, her hand resting on the "Sacred Things" box. "I did. I told her the roots held."

CHAPTER 34

THE CLASSROOM SILENCE

The school was empty, a sanctuary of still air and unhurried shadows. It was the quiet of a field lying fallow after the harvest, a necessary rest before the next season of tilling began.

The hum of fluorescent lights buzzed faintly above, a mechanical hymn that filled the void left by voices and footsteps. The faint, clinical scent of lemon cleaner still lingered from the janitor's morning routine, a scent of renewal that always reminded Crystal of a temple being prepared for its worshipers. She walked slowly through the hall, the rhythmic *click* of her heels on the polished floors sounding like a steady, deliberate heartbeat. Her steps weren't hurried today; she wasn't racing against a clock or chasing a deadline. Today was different. Classes were out for the week, the students off on their well-earned break, and the staff enjoying a rare long weekend. But Crystal had come in anyway. Not to work. Not to prep. Not to be the "Mama Crown" that everyone needed. She came just to feel the weight of the space she had built.

She passed the main office, giving a gentle glance toward the front desk where Lorraine usually stood as a joyful gatekeeper. In the silence, the desk felt like a story paused mid-sentence, waiting for the ink to dry. Crystal reached Classroom 3, her favorite room—the one where the wide windows acted as a frame for the world outside and the lighting turned soft and honey-hued in the late afternoons. She opened the door quietly, the hinges giving a soft, familiar sigh, and stepped inside.

The room greeted her with a hush so profound it felt like a physical embrace.

Desks were still arranged in intentional circles from the last group exercise, a testament to the community they were cultivating. The whiteboard held the fading remnants of a motivational quote she had written earlier that week, the ink a bit dusty but the message still sharp: *"You are worthy of more than just survival. You are worthy of joy. Your crown is secure because your roots are deep."*

Crystal walked to the back of the room and took a seat in a student chair. It was small, grounding, and humble. She let the silence stretch around her, wrapping it about her shoulders like a shawl.

It wasn't an empty silence; it was a sacred one.

This room had been a nursery for souls. It had held the salt of desperate tears and the lightning of breakthroughs. It had absorbed laughter that echoed off the walls like birdsong and the heavy, humid air of first-day jitters. Crystal closed her eyes, and in the quiet, she could almost hear the echoes of the transformation that had taken place within these four walls.

She remembered the girl who arrived late every day, her breath ragged because she had to drop off her little brother across town, yet her eyes always held a hunger for a better life. She remembered the young man who had barely spoken above a whisper, a sapling hidden in the shade, until the day he aced his clinicals and stood before the class with his head held high, finally seeing the man he was becoming. She thought of the mother who passed her exam on the third try—a late-season bloom that was all the more beautiful for its struggle—and how she had wept openly when she read the word *Congratulations* on the screen.

This room had seen them rise. And in the process, it had seen her rise, too.

Crystal folded her hands in her lap, her fingers interlaced as if in prayer, and breathed deeply. For years, she had lived under the heavy illusion that her value came only from the *doing*. From the achieving. From the relentless proving to a world that had once tried to uproot her. But this silence—this quiet, living moment—reminded her that presence was an offering in itself. Being here. Still. Whole. She was the root system beneath the school, and even when the tree was quiet, the roots were still doing the holy work of holding on.

She reached into her purse and pulled out her journal, the leather cover soft from the oil of her hands. Flipping to a fresh, blank page, she began to write, the pen moving with a rhythmic grace: *"Today, I sat in silence. No one needed my strength. No one called my name. And still, I mattered. Still, I belonged. I have built something that speaks of legacy even when I am quiet. My crown is not a burden; it is a rest."*

The afternoon sun began its slow descent, pouring through the windows and casting long, golden stripes across the desks like bars of light from a cathedral window. Crystal closed her eyes for a moment and leaned back in the small chair, letting the warmth soak into her skin.

The silence didn't feel empty. It felt like peace. It felt like the "well done" she had been waiting to hear from her own soul.

She stayed for a while longer, watching the dust motes dance in the light until the sun dipped lower and the day leaned toward the soft purple of evening. Then, she stood, tucked her journal away, and walked back through the hall.

Before leaving, she paused at the entryway. She didn't look back at the desks or the equipment, but at the spirit of the place.

The classroom was still. But the roots were deep, and the story was just beginning to bloom.

CHAPTER 35

THE SPEAKING INVITE

The auditorium was modest, a quiet sanctuary of learning tucked inside the community college where Crystal had once given a guest lecture in a season of much shorter shadows. This time, however, she hadn't come to fill a gap in a syllabus. She had been asked to serve as the keynote speaker for the annual "Leadership with Integrity" symposium—a title that felt like a harvest she had spent years tilling in the dark.

She arrived early.

It wasn't out of the frantic nerves that used to drive her, but out of a deep, prayerful reverence for what the moment signified. In her past life, she had often felt she had to fight for the light, to push her way through the canopy just to be seen. But today, the soil was different. She stood in the spotlight by invitation, not by force. She felt like a tree that had finally grown tall enough to provide shade, rather than just competing for sun.

The organizer, a kind-eyed woman named Dr. Monroe, greeted her near the heavy velvet curtains with a soft, genuine hug. "We wanted someone real, Crystal," she whispered, her voice carrying the weight of a woman who had seen many seasons herself. "We wanted someone who's lived the lesson in the fire, not just taught it from the safety of a textbook."

Crystal smiled, the expression reaching the corners of her eyes where the fine lines told the story of her resilience. "Then I guess I'm in the right place. The fire has a way of stripping away the performance until only the truth is left."

As she waited backstage, the muffled hum of the gathering crowd vibrating through the floorboards, she allowed her mind to wander back. The past no longer stung like a fresh wound, but it remained as the sturdy bark that protected her heart. She wouldn't weaponize her pain, nor would she use it to cast shadows on those who had wronged her. Instead, she would honor it as the very thing that had deepened her roots.

When her name was finally called, the applause began gently and grew into a steady rain of affirmation. She stepped onto the stage wearing a deep plum blouse—the color of late-harvest grapes—and charcoal slacks, holding nothing but a small, hand-lettered note card. She looked out at the sea of eager faces—students with eyes full of spring, faculty who had weathered many winters, and young leaders looking for a map through the wilderness.

She adjusted the microphone, the feedback a brief, sharp reminder of the world's noise, and then she began.

"Don't chase titles," she said, her voice a calm, steady current. "Chase truth. Titles are crowns made of paper that can be torn away by the first storm. Truth? Truth is a root of stone. It lasts long after the season ends."

She let the silence linger, allowing the words to settle like seeds into the hearts of her listeners.

"I built two schools. One collapsed when the loyalty it was built upon proved to be a hollow branch. The other? It stands today on the bedrock of truth. And I want to tell you why that matters. Because if you lead without integrity, you're not leading—you're merely performing. And the world is tired of performances. It is hungry for presence. It is hungry for leaders whose roots are deeper than their reach."

The room leaned in. The collective breath of the audience seemed to catch.

She spoke with a raw, gentle honesty about the winter of betrayal, the grueling work of rebuilding, and the quiet power of resilience. She spoke about the strength required to refrain from revenge, explaining that a tree doesn't grow taller by trying to overshadow its neighbor, but by reaching for the heavens. She told them how sometimes leadership meant walking alone through a cold season, and how the loneliest decisions—the ones made in the secret soil of the soul—are often the most necessary for the bloom to eventually come.

She ended her message with a whisper that carried to the very back of the hall:

"Forgiveness isn't a sign of weakness; it is the ultimate wisdom. It is the act of releasing the poison so your own fruit can stay sweet. And remember, integrity doesn't mean being a perfect, unblemished flower. It means being honest about the dirt you came from and the scars you carry."

The standing ovation that followed wasn't wild or performative. It didn't feel like the hollow applause of a crowd. It was grateful. It was the sound of a forest acknowledging a truth that had echoed through its own branches.

She had told the truth. And in the economy of the Spirit, truth always finds its way home.

CHAPTER 36

SEEING EMILY AGAIN

It was a rainy Saturday when it happened—the kind of day where the sky is the color of a faded bruise and the air feels saturated, as if the earth is taking a long, slow drink before the next season's bloom.

Crystal had driven into town to pick up a specialty order of herbal teas and hand-bound journals for the Crown & Root bookstore shelf. This was a small side project she'd cultivated to encourage her students to tend to their inner worlds with as much diligence as they gave their outer accomplishments. She believed that a career without a centered soul was like a tree with heavy branches and no taproot—destined to topple in the first high wind.

She was walking toward the exit of Magnolia Market, the brown paper bag tucked securely under her arm, her coat damp from the persistent Virginia drizzle. The scent of dried lavender and rain-slicked pavement followed her. She reached the threshold just as the automatic doors wheezed open with a mechanical sigh—and there she was.

Emily.

She was standing just a few feet away, a ghost from a previous life made flesh and bone. She was wearing jeans and a soft gray sweater that looked like a cloud. Her hair was slightly longer than Crystal remembered, but pulled back in that same practical, familiar way. Their eyes met immediately—a collision of histories in the middle of a grocery store entryway. For a split second, the world seemed to tilt, and everything else fell away.

It wasn't a rush of anger. It wasn't the sharp, jagged pierce of old pain. It was simply stillness—the quiet that settles over a forest after a fire has finally burned itself out and the ash has turned to soil.

Crystal didn't flinch. She didn't look away. Neither did Emily. They both paused—like two pages of a book caught in the same sudden breeze, unwilling to turn forward but unable to remain open on the same line.

There were no fireworks of resentment. There was no dramatic confrontation that demanded an audience. There were no words spoken to reopen wounds that had finally, through much prayer and pruning, closed into silver scars.

Instead, there was just the heavy, humbling realization that they had once loved the same mission, stood for the same people, and bled for the same vision. They had shared a crown, and then they had broken it. Now, they stood as quiet strangers on opposite ends of a story that had already been written.

Emily offered a soft, tentative nod—a small white flag of recognition.

Crystal returned it. Her posture was calm, her spirit certain, her heart unmoved. The "Mama Crown" in her didn't need to shout to be heard; she simply occupied her space with the quiet authority of a woman who knew her roots were deep.

And then, just like that, they passed one another. There were no smiles, but there were no scowls either. Just a holy kind of passage.

It was a quiet, sacred peace that didn't beg for resolution or an apology. It was the kind of freedom that comes when you've forgiven not just the person who uprooted you, but also the version of yourself that once believed you couldn't survive without their approval.

Crystal walked back to her car, the sky misting gently as if it, too, were exhaling a long-held breath. She didn't cry. She didn't replay the moment in her head, searching for things she should have said. She simply sat in the driver's seat for a few moments, watching the wipers clear the glass, her hands warm around the small bag of tea tucked in her coat pocket.

When she got home to the cottage, she placed the new journals on her desk. She opened one to a fresh, cream-colored page and let the ink flow: *We met again today. Not as enemies. Not even as friends. Just two women who shared a crown, cracked it, and chose different ways to rebuild. She is not my villain. She is just a part of the chapter I survived—the fire that prepared the soil for what I am growing now.*

Then she closed the journal. She had no intention of telling anyone about the encounter. Not even Lorraine. It was a secret tithe she paid to her own healing—a sealed moment, a final sigh in a story that no longer needed retelling.

That night, as she lay beneath the heavy weight of her quilt, her fingers brushed against the familiar texture of the embroidery. Her thumb traced the words stitched into the border: *"Every crown leaves roots."*

Crystal whispered a prayer—not for reconciliation, but for the beauty of the release.

"Thank You, God," she breathed into the darkness, "for letting me see her... and letting me realize I am finally, truly free."

CHAPTER 37

SUNDAY MORNING

The sky was unusually clear for a Sunday in early spring, a vast canopy of blue that looked as though it had been scrubbed clean of every winter cloud. The air was crisp but forgiving, warmed by a sun rising steadily behind the steeple of Grace Baptist Chapel—a small, white-clapboard sanctuary tucked beneath a gentle hill on the edge of town. It stood there like an old, sturdy tree that had survived many storms, its roots deep in the red Virginia clay.

Crystal hadn't planned on attending the service that morning.

She hadn't gone in a long while; her relationship with the church house had grown complicated over the years, a garden where both weeds and flowers had been allowed to grow unchecked. Once upon a time, she had sat on the front pew every Sunday, her Bible marked and highlighted until the pages were thin, scribbling notes as if they were the literal blueprints to becoming whole. But betrayal, exhaustion, and the relentless, crushing demands of life had turned her faith into a quiet, private sanctuary. It had become something she carried in her spirit rather than something she performed in a pew. For a long time, she had been protecting her roots in the dark, afraid the light of the sanctuary might burn what was left of her.

Still, something nudged her that morning—a soft, persistent tug at her soul that felt like the first stirring of a seed beneath the soil.

She found herself standing at her closet, her fingertips brushing against the cool fabric of the same cream-colored dress she hadn't worn since that final, bittersweet graduation ceremony at Crown Point Academy. She slipped it on slowly, the silk feeling like a second skin. It felt like remembering who she had once been and gently reintroducing herself to that version—the woman who believed in miracles before she knew the cost of them. When she arrived at the church, the floorboards creaked a familiar welcome. No one greeted her with fanfare or whispers. No one asked where she'd been or why she'd stayed away. And that was exactly what made it feel safe.

The sanctuary smelled of cedar wood, old hymnals, and the faint, sweet scent of floor wax.

A small choir sang with a raw, visceral harmony that needed no microphones or polished production. The rhythm section—a single drummer and a bass player—kept time on instinct, a heartbeat that pulsed through the wooden pews. Crystal sat in the middle row, her back straight and her palms resting open on her knees in a gesture of surrender. Her eyes remained fixed on the modest wooden cross above the pulpit, a reminder of the ultimate pruning that led to the ultimate life.

The sermon began in Genesis, drifting through the ancient dust of creation. But then, the pastor shifted.

"Let's talk about Joseph," he said, stepping down from the pulpit to pace slowly in front of the altar. "Let's talk about the jagged edge of betrayal. Let's talk about finding favor in unfamiliar, lonely places. Let's talk about what happens when God gives you the dream of a crown, but life hands you the reality of a pit."

Crystal inhaled sharply, the air catching in her chest like a sudden frost.

He continued, his voice dropping to a resonant, conversational tone. "Sometimes, the ones who throw you into that pit share your blood... or they share your table and your trust. Sometimes, the favor doesn't show up until after the damage is done. But hear me this morning—just because they didn't see your worth, doesn't mean God forgot your assignment. The pit is just a deeper place for your roots to take hold."

Crystal closed her eyes, letting the words wash over her like a warm spring rain.

"You might lose the coat," the pastor added, his voice rising with a holy fire, "but you'll never lose the calling. The coat was just the crown men could see, but the character was the root God was growing in the dark. God's favor isn't attached to the approval of people. And destiny still shows up—even in Egypt."

A single tear slid down her cheek, tracing a path through the light dusting of powder. Not a sob. Not a breakdown. Just a silent, sacred agreement between her heart and heaven.

"Your past was preparation," the pastor finished, his eyes seeming to find hers for a fleeting second. "Your betrayal was a push toward your purpose. And your silence? That was God holding space for the testimony you're about to give."

Crystal wept quietly then, her shoulders finally relaxing. She didn't weep in grief for what was stolen. She wept in gratitude for what had been preserved. She thanked God for every detour, every closed door, and every lonely mirror she'd had to face. She wept for the woman she used to be—the one who was afraid and overworked, needing the world to tell her she was a queen.

And she wept for the woman she had become—rooted, unbothered, and finally, beautifully whole.

After the service, as the congregation drifted toward the doors, an older woman with silver curls and skin like folded silk approached her in the aisle. "You have a light about you, daughter," she said gently, patting Crystal's hand. "I don't know your story. I don't know your name. But I felt your spirit today. Keep growing toward the sun."

Crystal smiled through damp lashes, her heart full. "Thank you," she whispered. "That means more than you know."

She walked out of the chapel slowly, the midday sunlight catching the gold threads of her dress. As she reached the stone steps, she paused and looked up into the vast, clear blue. She wasn't looking for answers anymore; she was simply offering a tithe of thanks.

"God, I'm not perfect," she breathed into the wind. "But I'm still here. And by Your grace, I'm still becoming. Thank You for never leaving my side—even when I almost left Yours."

The wind, cool and sweet, kissed her cheek like a benediction.

In that moment, Crystal didn't feel like someone who had been betrayed. She felt like someone who had been chosen. She felt like someone who had been preserved for a harvest she was finally ready to reap.

CHAPTER 38

The Proposal

It wasn't fireworks or fanfare that brought them together. It was conversation—quiet, intentional, and layered with the kind of sincerity that acted like a soothing balm on a scorched spirit. It was the kind of talk that made time slow down, tilling the hardened ground of the heart until the pain felt lighter and the possibilities felt green again. They had met during a local leadership summit, an event where Crystal had been asked to speak about the sacred work of resilience in education. She'd almost declined, the old whispers of inadequacy trying to take root in her mind once more. But something deep within—a still, small voice—had whispered, *"Go. There is a different kind of harvest waiting for you."*

His name was Malcolm.

He wasn't flashy or boastful, not the kind of man who needed to shout to be heard. He was a man with gentle, observant eyes and a voice that seemed to calm the very air around him. He had introduced himself with no hidden agenda, offering only a genuine curiosity that felt like cool water on a summer day.

"I really appreciated what you said about rebuilding," he had told her after her keynote, standing near the edge of the stage as the crowd thinned. "It takes more courage to start again from the roots than it does to start at all. You speak like a woman who knows the weight of her own crown."

They had exchanged business cards—nothing flirtatious, just a mutual, professional respect. But then came a thoughtful follow-up email. Then coffee at the small, sun-drenched café by the courthouse. Then long, meandering walks around the local botanical garden, where they spoke of seasons and growth. Then came dinners that stretched into hours, not because of the richness of the food, but because the company made even the simplest bread taste like a feast.

Malcolm was a widower, a retired Army engineer who had settled into the quiet labor of nonprofit work. He wasn't intimidated by Crystal's strength; he admired the way she carried her history. He listened when she spoke, even when her words were messy, or hesitant, or tangled in the briars of old grief.

"I'm not asking for a performance of perfection," he once told her as they sat on a park bench, the autumn leaves falling like gold coins around them. "Just honesty. And your presence. I want to know the roots, not just the bloom."

And for the first time in years, she felt safe enough to give him both.

They didn't rush. Love bloomed slowly, like a perennial that had survived a hard frost and was finally trusting the sun again. They went weeks without labels and months without heavy promises. But each shared moment grew more rooted in something tangible and real. One Saturday afternoon, Malcolm drove her out to a magnolia grove just beyond the next county line. The trees were ancient, stretching their branches wide like open arms offering sanctuary. Their thick, waxy white blooms framed the path like a gallery of living art.

He parked under the largest tree, the scent of the blossoms—heavy and sweet—filling the car. He walked around to open her door, his movements steady and sure.

"This was my wife's favorite place," he said softly, his voice echoing with a tender history. "When she passed, I used to come here and talk to God until the sun went down. For a long time, I didn't think I'd ever want to invite another soul into this grove. I didn't think I'd love again. And I had made my peace with that. But then I met you, Crystal."

Crystal's breath caught, the air in her lungs feeling like a prayer.

He reached into his coat pocket and pulled out a small, navy velvet box. He didn't stand over her; he stood with her.

"I don't want to complete you, Crystal. I don't believe in that. You've been whole for a long time, and you've built a kingdom on your own terms. What I'm asking is different."

He knelt then, not out of empty ceremony, but out of a deep, grounded truth.

"I'm not asking you to step down from your throne or lower your standards. I'm asking if I can walk the grounds with you. Will you let me build peace by your side?"

Crystal's eyes filled with tears—not the jagged tears of betrayal she had known before, but the soft, overflowing rain of gratitude. She didn't speak right away. She didn't need to. In the silence of the grove, her spirit had already answered.

She knelt beside him—gently, slowly, letting her dress settle into the grass—and pressed her forehead to his. She whispered a single word: "Yes."

It wasn't the kind of "yes" that expected him to fix her past. It was the kind of "yes" that said she was finally ready to be loved softly. Without the need for control. Without the suffocating weight of conditions. It was a "yes" that offered respect and demanded room to breathe.

They sat there together under the shade of the magnolia, as the sun filtered through the waxy leaves, dabbing the earth with light. For a long moment, time stood still.

Later, she would call Lorraine to share the news. Later, she would tell her son, Deon, that her heart had found a new anchor. But in that moment, she simply rested her head on Malcolm's shoulder and closed her eyes, letting her soul exhale in a way it never had before.

She had been burned by fire, broken by betrayal, and buried by the weight of expectations. And yet, here she was, blooming in a different soil.

She was chosen—not because she needed a savior to rescue her, but because she was finally, truly seen. The crown was no longer a burden of loyalty; it was a gift of grace.

CHAPTER 39

MARRIED, NOT MUZZLED

It was not a cathedral wedding. There were no gold-draped aisles, no showy processions orchestrated to impress a crowd of strangers. There were no flower girls rehearsing measured steps or reception halls lit like movie sets to mask a hollow center. I had spent too much of my life performing in rooms where the lighting was artificial, where the glare blinded people to the truth of the shadows.

It was a garden. Simple. Open. Introspective and intentionally alive.

The morning sun draped the grass in warm, honeyed light—a celestial benediction that felt far more sacred than the filtered glow of any stained glass. I stood barefoot on the cool stone pathway, feeling the steady pulse of the earth beneath my arches. It was a physical reminder that I was finally, truly grounded. I was surrounded by a small, hand-picked circle of people who mattered: a few loyal friends whose hands had helped me till the hard ground of my grief, my son, Malcolm's grown daughter, and Miss Lila, who stood as sturdy as an elder oak, holding a bundle of lavender and baby's breath that perfumed the breeze with the scent of restoration.

I wore a white cotton dress—flowing, effortless, and unencumbered. I chose no veil to hide my eyes from the truth, no layers to separate me from the wind. My curls were pinned back loosely, and a delicate crown of baby's breath circled my head. It sat lightly upon my brow; it was a crown of peace instead of a crown of pressure, a symbol of truth instead of a burden of tradition. I wasn't hiding behind the heavy mask of makeup or the rigid, suffocating structures of ceremony.

I had arrived as I was. In the eyes of God and this small company, I was a woman who had survived the pruning and was finally allowed to bloom on her own terms. And that was more than enough.

Malcolm stood beneath the cedar arbor, waiting with a patience that felt like an anchor in a restless sea. His gray suit was simple, and his shoes were slightly dusty from walking the same grass that had brought us to this moment. When he saw me, his smile widened—not merely because I was stunning, though I felt a radiance I hadn't known in years, but because I had shown up fully as myself, with my scars and my strength in plain view.

"I told you I'd never try to fix you," he said softly as I reached his side, his hands reaching for mine. His grip was warm, steady, and certain.

"And I told you I'd never shrink again," I whispered back, a vow made in the quiet of my own soul long before we reached this altar.

We held hands as the officiant—Malcolm's cousin and a longtime pastor—opened his Bible to the passage about love not being boastful or proud. But before he could begin the formal liturgy, I gently raised my hand. I felt a nudge from the Spirit, a sacred need to testify.

"I want to say something," I said, my voice clear and steady as a mountain stream cutting through stone.

There was a holy pause, a hush that settled over the garden, and then I turned to those gathered.

"I was told, once, that love would make me smaller. I was taught by the world that I needed to bend until I broke just to be accepted—that I had to be less of a woman to be loved more by a partner. For a long time, I believed that lie. I let my roots wither while I tried to keep a fake crown polished for the sake of a loyalty that didn't love me back."

My eyes met Malcolm's, and I saw only the reflection of my own worth.

"But this man never asked me to shrink. He didn't want to dim my fire; he wanted to sit by the flame and understand its source. He's not here to complete me, because he knows the Lord made me whole long before our paths crossed. He's here to walk with me. To listen to the silence and the song. To build a legacy that doesn't require me to bury my voice or muzzle my spirit."

I turned back to Malcolm, tears dancing in my lashes like morning dew.

"So today, I say yes—not to ownership, for I belong only to the Creator. Not to being tamed, for my spirit was meant to be wild and free. But I say yes to partnership. To laughter that heals the deep places. To quiet that restores the weary soul. To growing together in the same rich soil. I say yes to being fully me, without apology."

Malcolm's turn came next, and his voice was as solid as a sturdy oak.

"I don't want to save you, Crystal. You've already saved yourself through the grace you've claimed. I just want to serve beside you. To be your peace when the wind picks up. To be your mirror when you forget your light. To be your home."

We didn't recite vows from a dusty book of traditions. We spoke what we knew to be true in the marrow of our bones. And when the words were done, and the pastor pronounced us husband and wife, I leaned in—not with the trembling of a girl seeking a rescue, but with the trust of a woman who had found a teammate.

Our kiss wasn't a dramatic performance for the cameras. It was gentle, patient, and slow. It was love that had done the hard work of healing first.

The guests clapped softly, a rhythmic sound like rain on summer leaves. Miss Lila wiped her eyes with a lace handkerchief and whispered loud enough for the angels to hear, "That's how queens marry—when they've reclaimed their thrones and honored their roots."

Later, there was no loud reception or choreographed dance floor. Instead, there was a long wooden table set beneath the sprawling, protective branches of a magnolia tree. It was filled with casseroles, iced tea, and the rich, nourishing sound of laughter and stories.

My son, Deon, stood up to give a toast, his eyes shining with a pride that matched my own.

"Ma, I've watched you rebuild. I've seen you pull yourself up from nothing, from betrayal, from a grief that would have buried anyone else. You didn't just find love again—you found your freedom. And today, you reminded me that real love doesn't cage the bird to keep it. It crowns the bird and lets it fly. I'm proud of you."

I smiled through tears that felt like a spring thaw.

I was married. But I was not muzzled. This wasn't just a new chapter in an old story. It was an entirely new volume, written in my own resilient voice, on my own sacred terms. I had learned that when loyalty costs you your soul, the price is too high—but when loyalty is rooted in truth, the harvest is beyond anything you can imagine.

CHAPTER 40

A Place Called Home

They didn't go house hunting in a big city. There were no gated communities to navigate, no smart-home tours with programmed lights, and no glossy, polished brochures promising a life of curated perfection. Crystal had already lived in a house of cards that looked like a palace; this time, she was looking for a foundation that reached the bedrock.

Instead, Crystal and Malcolm drove with the windows down through winding back roads and shaded, wooded lanes. The air smelled of damp pine needles and wild clover. They stopped whenever something felt right—even if it didn't look like much to a passing eye. Crystal was learning to trust the pull of her spirit over the logic of a blueprint.

They found it on a high hill just outside the county line. Five acres of wild, unruly land. Untouched. Unclaimed.

The grass was knee-high in places, swaying like a green sea in the breeze. A crumbling stone fence, gray and gritty with age, wound along the property's edge like a forgotten boundary. But the ancient oaks on the ridge whispered stories of endurance, and beneath her feet, the earth felt... faithful. It felt like soil that had been waiting for someone to treat it with kindness.

"I can see it," Crystal said softly, stepping out of the truck and into the wind, letting it pull at her hair. "Not just a house—but a place of peace. A sanctuary for the soul."

Malcolm nodded, his hand finding the small of her back, steady as an anchor. "Then let's build it from the soil up. No shortcuts. Just truth."

And they did. Together.

It took months of patient labor. There were permits to sign, plans to redraw, inevitable delays, and the quiet compromises that come when two lives are being grafted into one.

But every delay felt like a season of rest, and every compromise was a lesson in grace. It was theirs.

The house was not grand by magazine standards. It had no cold marble foyer or sweeping spiral staircase. But it had wide, deep porches that wrapped around the structure like open arms, inviting the world to sit a while. There was a swing Malcolm hung himself, the chains creaking a rhythmic lullaby in the evenings. The kitchen featured open shelving for her favorite collection of mismatched mugs—each one a memory of a different town, a different lesson. In the living room, a fireplace stood with a mantel carved from an old, weathered barn beam they had rescued from a demolition site. It was scarred and beautiful, a piece of wood that had survived the collapse and found a new purpose.

The bookshelves—Malcolm built them into the very bones of every room. Crystal filled them with volumes of poetry, books of faith, memoirs of survivors, and a growing, sacred stack of her own journals.

There was a small, sun-drenched study where she could write her heart onto the page. A music corner where Malcolm played jazz on Saturday mornings, the notes drifting through the house like incense. And a sunroom with windows on all sides where the light poured in like liquid grace, illuminating the dust motes as they danced.

In the backyard, Crystal planted a tree. An oak sapling. Sturdy. Young. Full of promise. At its base, she placed a small wooden sign with hand-etched words that she had carved herself: *"The Root of Everything That Lasted."*

Every evening, they sat on the porch, watching the sky change colors like a living painting, shifting from the fire of sunset to the cool indigo of dusk. Sometimes they talked about the students at the school or the dreams for the coming year. Sometimes they just listened to the wind. Sometimes, peace sounds like nothing at all.

One morning, she wandered barefoot through the hallway in her robe, sipping a cup of warm chamomile. The hardwood floors were honey-colored and warm from the morning sun, and music played low from a speaker tucked behind a leafy philodendron. She paused at the front door.

On the inside of the doorframe, she had hung a small wooden plaque. Malcolm hadn't seen her do it yet. It was her private declaration. It read: *"Here we live crowned, not caged."*

She touched the plaque gently, her fingers tracing the letters, then pressed her palm to her heart. There were no ghosts haunting these hallways. No echoes of betrayal trapped in the corners. No rushing to meet someone else's expectations. No proving her worth to a world that didn't know her name.

Just presence. Just the deep, quiet joy of being known and still being loved.

Months later, her son came to visit with his new partner. They walked the land together, laughing and barefoot, careless in the best way. At dinner, as the steam rose from the bowls of stew, he looked around the table, then at his mother. He saw the way she sat—shoulders relaxed, head held high, eyes clear.

"You're not just surviving anymore, Ma," he said, his voice thick with pride. "You're rooted."

Crystal smiled, a slow, radiant bloom of a smile.

"Yes," she replied, her voice full and soft. "I finally came home to myself. I found the soil I was meant for."

CHAPTER 41

PAGES AND PAGES

The idea didn't descend like a lightning strike—loud, jagged, and startling. It didn't arrive in a sudden burst of brilliance that demanded the world's attention. Instead, it arrived in the quiet, much like the first determined sprout of a seed that has finally decided to break through the dark, cool earth.

It was one of those late autumn evenings where the world feels as though it is exhaling. The fire crackled low in the hearth, sending a comforting scent of charred hickory and cedar through the room. I sat curled in my writing chair, my body enveloped in the heavy, hand-stitched warmth of the quilt Miss Lila had given me—the one that reminded me that even mismatched scraps can make something beautiful when they are held together with purpose. Outside, the dry leaves rustled against the windowpane like soft, distant applause from a forest that had seen me survive the winter. Inside, the only sound was the patient hum of the laptop and the rhythmic thrum of my own heart.

My fingers hovered over the keyboard. There were no looming deadlines, no publisher expectations to satisfy, and no hollow ambitions for viral fame. There was only a persistent, gentle nudge in my spirit—the "Calm Mentor" within finally finding her voice. It was a whisper that felt like a command: *"Tell them what saved you. Tell them about the roots."*

So, I started.

At first, the words were scattered, like fallen leaves caught in a whirlwind. I pulled from a decade of memories, hard-won lessons, and phrases I had scribbled on faded Post-it notes and in the tear-stained margins of my journals over the years. I typed without filters or fear of judgment. I wrote as if I were speaking directly to a room full of women who had been betrayed, abandoned, silenced, or misunderstood—women who felt like their own crowns had been stolen or crushed in the dirt.

I wasn't writing for praise. I was writing for the woman in her lowest, loneliest moment—the one sitting in her car outside a building she had to walk away from, her hands gripping the steering wheel, her breath hitched with the salt of a thousand unshed tears. I was writing for the woman who stared into the mirror and didn't recognize the ghost looking back. I was writing for her, because I *was* her.

The chapters emerged like a slow, steady healing—uneven and raw, but firm as stone.

Chapter 1: You Are Still Worthy of the Soil.

Chapter 2: Let the Fire Teach, Not Consume.

Chapter 3: Rebuilding Doesn't Mean Repeating the Same Cracks.

Chapter 4: Crown Yourself Again—This Time, From Within.

By week six, the screen showed nearly 40,000 words. They were words forged in the fire and cooled by the waters of peace. I printed a draft, the printer's mechanical whirring sounding like a long-held breath finally released. I placed the stack on my desk and flipped through the pages slowly. Some were indeed tear-stained, the ink slightly blurred where my past had met my present. Others were marked with frantic, hopeful notes in the margins: *"Say more here about the silence,"* or *"This one will break her open—then finally, finally free her."*

I titled it: *Beneath the Crown: When Loyalty Cost Too Much – A Guide for Women Rebuilding from Betrayal, Burnout, and Brokenness.*

I didn't call it a memoir. This wasn't a project of nostalgia or a petty exercise in score-settling. This was a survival manual wrapped in the soft, protective skin of storytelling. I included journal prompts that demanded honesty and reflection questions that reached into the deep places. I added the soft, fierce affirmations I once needed to hear when I was drowning:

"You are not too late; your season is just beginning."

"What left you wasn't your fault. But what stays is your choice."

"Love again—but guard the roots of your soul this time."

When I read through the final draft, I didn't feel like an author seeking a platform. I felt like a messenger delivering a map to those still lost in the woods.

One afternoon, as the sun dipped below the hills, I walked out to the oak tree I had planted. The bark was rough and cool beneath my palm, the trunk growing thicker and more certain with every passing month. I placed my hand against it, feeling the life within, and whispered into the wind: "Let this book be shade for someone who never had cover. Let it be the water for a thirsty heart."

Then I returned to my desk, the glow of the lamp feeling like a sacred light. I opened a new file and began writing the introduction, my voice steady and sure:

If you are reading this, you've probably lost something that mattered. Maybe it was a friend you trusted with your secrets, a business you built with your sweat, a dream that felt like home, or even the very sense of who you are. I want you to know: this is not the end of your forest. In fact, it might be the beginning of everything that will truly last. You're not broken; you're being tilled. You're not falling; you're being planted. And crowns, my love, are forged in the fire—never merely gifted.

CHAPTER 42

THE DAY SHE FORGOT THE PAIN

It began like any other day, a quiet unfolding of light that didn't demand a single thing from me.

There was no particular occasion marked in ink, no celebration circled in red on the kitchen calendar. It was just a golden Saturday morning, the kind that tiptoes in gently through the linen curtains, humming a soft, amber light into every corner of the house. Crystal rose with the sun, her movements slow and intentional, a dance of peace she had finally mastered. She brewed her coffee—the aroma of dark beans and chicory filling the kitchen like an old friend—and went to feed the birds just outside the window. She laughed softly to herself as two cardinals squabbled over a perch on the feeder, their tiny wings flapping with the frantic energy of gossiping sisters. She opened the windows wide, letting the Virginia breeze wash through the rooms like a fresh anointing, clearing out the last remnants of the night's shadows. There was no heaviness in her chest today.

There was no invisible weight pressing on her shoulders, no phantom crown of thorns demanding her attention.

She didn't realize it at first—how different the very air felt in her lungs. She just knew she wanted music, a soundtrack for a soul finally at rest. She turned on her favorite playlist: a warm blend of old-school R&B, a few soaring gospel tracks, and the jazz instrumentals she had discovered on a rainy Tuesday months ago. She swayed while sweeping the hardwood floors, her broom keeping time with the bass. She sang while folding the laundry, her voice steady and clear. She even danced a little while washing the breakfast dishes, the soap bubbles catching the light like tiny, fleeting prisms.

By noon, the house smelled of home. She had baked a pan of sweet cornbread and fried a few pieces of catfish, just because the spirit moved her. It wasn't for company, and it wasn't to fill a void of comfort. It was simply a celebration of the present moment.

She FaceTimed her son, Deon, who answered with a wide, bright smile that made her heart swell like a rising tide. He was thriving overseas—training hard, laughing often, and already asking about the next time she'd fly over to see him play.

"Soon," she promised, leaning her chin on her hand as she watched his face on the screen. "I'm so proud of you, Deon. You're standing so tall."

He grinned, his eyes reflecting the strength she had poured into him. "Only because I'm yours, Ma. My roots go deep because of you."

After the call, she walked out to the garden to check on the progress of the season. The hydrangeas, which had struggled through the previous frost, were finally blooming again in clusters of vibrant blue and soft lavender. She knelt in the dirt, the soil cool against her knees, and cupped one of the heavy blossoms in her hands.

"You came back," she whispered, her voice a soft caress.

Perhaps she wasn't just talking to the flower. She was acknowledging the woman who had also pushed through the frozen ground to find the sun.

Later that afternoon, a former student named Tasha dropped by unexpectedly, her two young children trailing behind her like ducklings. They brought a mason jar filled with warm banana pudding and exciting updates about Tasha's new position at a local clinic.

"You gave me more than a career, Ms. Crystal," the young woman said, her eyes glistening with a sudden, raw sincerity. "You gave me back my identity. You showed me I wasn't just a victim of my past, but a queen in training."

Crystal hugged her tightly, feeling the strength in the young woman's frame. It was the hug of a mentor who had seen the harvest.

It wasn't until the door finally closed and the velvet quiet of the evening settled back into the house that the realization hit her like a sudden, beautiful bolt of lightning.

She hadn't thought about the pain all day.

Not once.

She hadn't thought about the betrayal that had once felt like a permanent scar. She hadn't thought about the loss of the first school or the stinging words that had been hurled her way. She hadn't thought about the versions of herself that had withered and died under someone else's cruel decisions. She sat on the couch, stunned by the sheer lightness of her own spirit.

Then slowly—deliberately—she whispered into the stillness of the room:

"God... thank You. I truly didn't think I'd ever get here."

The words weren't a desperate shout. They didn't come from a place of grief or the frantic need for rescue. They rose up from a deep, settled place. A place that had once been scorched and blackened by disillusionment and doubt, but had now grown soft with peace. Fertile with gratitude. Rooted in grace.

She cried then, but the tears were different. These were tears of arrival. They were the tears of a woman remembering who she was before the heartbreak—and recognizing that somehow, through the ashes and the aftershocks, she had become someone even more whole, even more resilient than before.

She had forgotten the pain—not because it didn't matter, and not because it hadn't happened, but because it no longer managed her joy. It no longer held the keys to her kingdom. It no longer defined the room she entered or the way she saw her reflection in the glass. The pain had become just a chapter in a very long book. It was a footnote. It was not the story.

She lit a single candle, its flame a steady golden pulse. She sat with her journal and wrote the final lines of a season:

"Today, I laughed without searching the corners of the room for the ghosts of my wounds. Today, I danced without waiting for anyone else's permission to be happy. Today, I remembered who I was before the pain named me. And I liked her. She's still in here—wiser now, deeper now, and finally, finally free. The roots held. The crown is light."

CHAPTER 43

THE CROWN REBUILT

The classroom was quiet—an expectant, holy hush that felt like a field resting just before the first light of spring. Early morning sun stretched across the freshly polished floors in long, golden fingers, touching every desk like a silent blessing.

Crystal stood at the front of the room, her back to the door, watching the sunlight settle into the corners. A soft hum of anticipation lingered in the air, a vibration she felt in the soles of her feet, though the students hadn't yet arrived. The whiteboard was a clean slate, waiting for the ink of new dreams. The seats were empty, yet the atmosphere was charged with a heavy, beautiful promise. It was the kind of silence that didn't feel like an absence, but a presence.

She adjusted the chair behind the instructor's desk—a sturdy, oak piece that felt more like a throne than any corporate leather chair she had ever sat in. She smoothed the fabric of her blouse, centered herself in the stillness, and walked to the window.

Outside, in the shared lot below, the world was waking up. A young woman was carefully practicing parallel parking—a first-time commuter student whose hands, Crystal knew, were likely trembling on the steering wheel. Two young men were already at the front door, their breath visible in the crisp morning air as they compared notes and laughed. She could hear the faint, muffled sound of their voices; they were joking about how dental terminology sounded like a foreign language. Crystal smiled, a deep, knowing warmth spreading through her.

Crown & Root had survived its growing pains. It had matured beyond a mere business venture into something far more ancient and enduring—a sanctuary. It was a school, certainly, but it was also a nursery where broken things weren't discarded as refuse; they were repurposed.

Replanted.

Rebuilt.

She walked slowly between the rows of desks, running her hand along the cool, smooth edge of each one. Every seat held a ghost of a story she carried in her heart: the mother of three who had studied by candlelight during night shifts; the veteran whose eyes had once been haunted but now looked toward the future; the quiet girl who had once whispered, through tears, that this class was the first time she felt she belonged to herself.

Each story was a thread in the tapestry. Each name was a seed she had watered. And she had been granted the sacred honor of witnessing the bloom.

She reached her own desk and picked up the leather-bound attendance book. It was old-fashioned, its cover smelling of deep woods and tobacco—intentionally so. In a world of digital clouds and fleeting data, something about writing each student's name by hand felt like a tithe. It was personal. It was an acknowledgment that they existed.

She flipped to the page for the new term.

Twenty-three names.

Twenty-three new chances for the soil to bring forth life.

She closed her eyes and whispered a prayer under her breath, her voice a soft cadence against the morning light. "God, let me serve them well. Let me lead with a heart that remembers the fire. Let this be more than a curriculum—let it be a confirmation of their purpose."

Her gaze drifted upward to the scripture framed above the whiteboard, the ink bold and unwavering: *"For what shall it profit a man, if he shall gain the whole world, and lose his own soul?" — Mark 8:36*

She had nearly lost her own soul once. She had been a woman chasing good intentions that had become entangled with the briars of pride and a blind, misplaced loyalty. She had built an empire of gold and glass, only to watch it fracture and fall because the roots hadn't been deep enough to hold the weight of the crown.

But through the ash, she had learned a lesson that no success could have taught her: some crowns aren't stolen by enemies. Some are shed by the spirit because they've become too heavy with the world's expectations.

And when you rebuild a crown from the soil of truth, it doesn't just sit precariously on your head. It grows from within, anchored by roots that no storm can reach.

A rhythmic knock sounded at the door.

Alicia, her assistant director, peeked in, her face glowing with the shared energy of the morning. "They're beginning to line up in the hallway, Ms. Crystal. You ready to open the gates?"

Crystal turned, her eyes soft with peace but steady with power. "I've been ready for a long time, Alicia."

She stepped out into the hallway, the sound of her heels a confident, grounded beat on the floor. The students stood waiting—a forest of young saplings. Some were nervous, shifting from foot to foot; others were excited, dressed in borrowed scrubs that were a size too large; many held their new notebooks clutched to their chests like shields against a world that had told them they wouldn't make it. They looked at her with awe. With hope.

With the heavy, beautiful expectation of the lost looking for a map.

She met their gazes without hesitation, her presence a calm anchor for their storm. And in a voice that was both a velvet caress and a pillar of strength, she said:

"Welcome to Crown & Root. We don't just train your hands here. We remind you of the royalty you've always carried in your soul."

There was no sudden applause. No dramatic music swelled to fill the space. There was only a quiet, holy silence that settled over the hallway—a moment wrapped in the kind of truth that changes the way a person breathes.

Crystal smiled again—this time fully, deeply, without the shadow of the past looming over her. Because she realized the greatest miracle wasn't the rebuilding of a school, but the rebuilding of the woman standing at its helm.

The girl who had once folded flyers in the rain, desperate for a chance, had become the woman who held the space for others to transform. The woman who had been betrayed now taught others how to lead with an integrity that could not be bought. The teacher who had once wept in an empty, darkened office now walked boldly into the light of her calling.

This was her redemption.

This was her crown.

Rebuilt, rooted, and fitting better than it ever had before.

EPILOGUE

LESSON 44

The morning of her forty-fourth birthday arrived with no loud fanfare, no frantic alarms, and no performative celebrations.

There were no clusters of balloons bobbing against the ceiling, and no digital countdown on a social media feed to announce her entry into a new year of life. Instead, the world offered a simpler, more sacred initiation. There was the clear, rhythmic birdsong weaving through the open window, the spicy, warming scent of cinnamon tea steeping in the kitchen, and a steady, quiet vibration of gratitude humming through her very marrow. Crystal stood in front of the bathroom mirror, her hands resting on the cool porcelain of the sink, studying her reflection with the eyes of a woman who had finally learned to be her own best friend.

The woman looking back was no longer the girl who used to shrink her spirit to fit into the small, cramped spaces of others' comfort. She was no longer the wounded co-founder, her voice hoarse from begging for a fairness the world wasn't ready to give. She was no longer the starving dreamer, waiting by the gate for a validation that only she could truly grant herself.

She was softer now—like soil after a long, necessary rain—but she was undeniably stronger. She was gentler in her touch, yet firmer in her boundaries. She was wiser, seasoned by the frost, but her heart remained as curious as a seedling reaching for the first light of dawn.

There were lines etched beneath her eyes now, fine and graceful. They were the topography of a life well-lived—proof that she had cried rivers of grief, laughed until the sun rose, healed through the fire, and survived the uprooting. Her hands bore callouses, too. They weren't from the physical labor of stacking bricks or hewing wood, but from the spiritual toil of tilling a life from lessons rather than losses. They were the hands of a woman who had learned how to hold onto her peace even when the wind tried to snatch it away.

She reached into the back of the small vanity drawer and pulled out a yellowed, folded piece of paper. It was a relic from ten years ago, written during the winter of her soul—the hardest year she had ever endured. On it were only three words, penned in a shaky but defiant hand: *Still becoming. Always.*

Crystal looked at those words, her thumb tracing the ink. She smiled at the ghost of the woman she used to be and whispered to the stillness, "You were right, honey. The growth never ends."

Then, with hands that were steady and sure, she pulled out a fresh sheet of stationery and a pen. She sat at her small writing desk, the morning sun painting gold stripes across the wood. She began to write a new letter—not a plea for help this time, but a lighthouse for her future self.

Lesson 44:

A crown is not a prize you win or a gift you are granted by the hands of men. It is not a shiny accessory meant to sit precariously on your head while you tremble, fearing it might fall. A true crown is a posture of the soul. It is the dignity you carry when you realize that your worth is not a business deal, and your value is not a negotiation.

If you want to wear the crown, you must first honor the root. You must be willing to go deep into the quiet, dark places where no one sees you, and anchor yourself in the Truth. Loyalty is a sacred currency; do not spend it on soil that refuses to let you bloom. Do not plant your heart in a garden where you are required to remain a seed so that others may feel like trees.

You are the gardener of your own peace. You have survived the fire, and now you are the flame. Stand tall, keep your roots deep, and remember: you don't need a throne to be royalty. You just need to be whole.

REFLECTION QUESTIONS FOR YOUR OWN REBUILDING JOURNEY

APPENDIX: THE SOIL OF REFLECTION

1. The Weight of Trust Think about a time when someone you deeply trusted disappointed or betrayed you. What did that experience teach you about the difference between loyalty and blind faith?

2. The Crown You Wore for Others Have you ever built something, achieved something, or become someone primarily to earn the approval of others? What parts of that "crown" were truly yours, and what parts were performance?

3. Naming the Loss Beyond the surface event, what did your hardest season actually cost you? Consider not just what you lost, but who you were before it happened. What version of yourself did you have to grieve?

4. The Letter You Never Sent If you could write a letter to someone who hurt you, one you never intend to send, what would you say? What would it feel like to release those words onto paper and then let them go?

5. Roots vs. Recognition Crystal learns that crowns without roots have no legacy. In your own life, what "roots" have you neglected while chasing visible success? What would it look like to tend to them now?

6. Your Soil After the Storm After a season of loss or betrayal, what remains in you that is still good, still true, still plantable? What seeds of purpose survived the fire?

7. Forgiveness as a Boundary The book presents forgiveness not as a bridge that invites people back, but as a boundary that sets you free. Is there someone you need to forgive, not for their sake, but to release yourself from carrying them?

8. The Silence That Heals Crystal finds peace in stillness, in moments where no one needed her and she simply existed. When was the last time you allowed yourself to be silent, unproductive, and still? What might that silence reveal if you gave it room?

9. Who You Are When You Stop Building If you stopped achieving, producing, or proving tomorrow, who would you be? What parts of your identity exist independent of your work, your titles, or your roles?

10. The People Who Stayed In your hardest season, who showed up for you without agenda? How did their presence shape your healing, and have you told them what their steadiness meant?

11. Rebuilding vs. Repeating When you start over, do you tend to rebuild the same structures that fell, or do you design something new? What patterns from your past do you want to intentionally leave behind this time?

12. Your Scripture on the Wall Crystal hangs a verse that anchors her mission: "What does it profit a man to gain the whole world, yet forfeit his soul?" What truth, scripture, or phrase would you hang on your wall to remind you of what matters most?

13. Love After the Breaking If past pain has made you guarded, what would it take for you to trust again, not recklessly, but wisely? What does healthy love look like on the other side of heartbreak?

14. The Legacy You Want to Leave Imagine someone writes about your life after you are gone. What do you want them to say about how you treated people, what you built, and how you handled the hard seasons? Are you living that story now?

15. Still Becoming Crystal ends her journey not as a finished product but as someone "still becoming." What are you still becoming? What growth remains ahead of you, and how does it feel to know your story is not yet complete?

Closing Invitation:

These questions are not meant to be answered in one sitting. Return to them as you walk your own rebuilding journey. Write in the margins. Sit with the discomfort. And remember: you are not behind. You are not too late. You are right on time.

A LEGACY OF LOVE

FAMILY SHOUTOUTS

From Dy (Oldest Child)

"Mom, being your oldest child has given me the opportunity to watch you grow. You trusted me first, loved me first, and taught me first what it means to be strong, responsible, and full of love. I watched you sacrifice, struggle, pray, and still show up for us every single day. Because of you, I learned how to lead, how to love deeply, and how to keep going even when life gets hard. Everything I am is rooted in observing you. Thank you for showing me how to be strong enough to carry love, lessons, and light for the ones who came after me. I love you always." □

—Dy

From Derrick Sharpe (Husband)

"A loving wife, mother, and a strong woman who always does the best for her family. I love you with all my heart. A true believer in doing what is right. My true friend who is with me through the good and bad. Those characteristics I truly admire about you, so keep going for your dreams and LOVE YOU!!!" □

—Derrick Sharpe

From Demerica Sharpe (Child)

"Momma, you are my greatest inspiration in life, the true example of a mother, a friend, and a wife. You've taught me how to be a loving and patient mother to my own child, how to love myself, and how to be confident in who I am. Every day, you strive to become a better version of yourself, even when it feels like the world is against you. I am the mother

I am today because I've watched and learned from you my entire life. You've shown me what it means to stay true to yourself, no matter what others think. I love you deeply, and I am beyond proud to call you my mom." □
—**Demerica Sharpe**

From Dayron Sharpe (Child)

"Ma, you was always a hero and inspiration in my eyes. You taught me what it was to keep going no matter if the cards in your favor, or if it feels like the whole weight of the world was on your shoulders. Without you I don't know what type of man I will be. You taught me what it means to sacrifice even if it doesn't benefit you. I am the human being I am for the way you raised me and I wouldn't replace it for the world. Thank you for always being my rock and my backbone through thick and thin. I wouldn't have made this far without you." □
—**Dayron Sharpe**

From Develle Sharpe (Child)

"My mother is an amazing person. She is very hardworking, full of energy, and kind. She always puts her children before anything. She is understanding, takes things slow, actually listens and helps me, my siblings, basically anyone with what they need. She tries to help everyone as much as she can. She really is a busy person but she never misses anything. She makes sure everyone else is okay before herself. She really is the kindest." □
—**Develle Sharpe**

ABOUT THE AUTHOR

Michelle Crumble-Sharpe is an entrepreneur, educator, and visionary storyteller from North Carolina. With a background in healthcare management, cosmetology, and workforce education, she blends her passion for service with her gift for storytelling. Her debut novel, Beneath the Crown: When Loyalty Cost Too Much, is a deeply personal reflection on friendship, ambition, betrayal, and healing.

Michelle's journey as an author is rooted in her own life experiences—rebuilding after loss, rediscovering purpose, and learning that loyalty without wisdom can become a costly crown to carry. Through her writing, she hopes to inspire readers to embrace self-worth, faith, and resilience, no matter how heavy their journey becomes.

When she's not writing, Michelle helps lead several ventures, including projects in business development, education, transportation, real estate, community outreach, and entertainment—each inspired by her belief that growth, like healing, begins at the root.

She resides in Greenville, North Carolina, and is the wife of Derrick Sharpe, and the proud mother of four: Dysheonia Pender (singer-songwriter Dyverxe), Day'Ron Sharpe (professional basketball player), Demerica Sharpe, and Develle Sharpe.